I0646997

HELEN ROW TOEWS

THE
RESISTANCE

VINCI
BOOKS

By Helen Row Toews

Runestaff Chronicles

The Awakening
The Resistance
The Legacy
The Secret

Vinci Books

vinci-books.com

Published by Vinci Books Ltd in 2025

1

Copyright © Helen Row Toews 2021

The author has asserted their moral right to be identified as the author of this work in accordance with the Copyright, Designs and Patents Act 1988. This work is a work of fiction. Names, characters, places and incidents are the product of the author's imagination or are used fictitiously. Any resemblance to actual persons, living or dead, places and incidents is entirely coincidental.

All rights reserved. No part of this publication may be copied, reproduced, distributed, stored in any retrieval system, or transmitted in any form or by any means, including photocopying, recording, or other electronic or mechanical methods, nor used as a source for any form of machine learning including AI datasets, without the prior written permission of the publisher.

The publisher and the author have made every effort to obtain permissions for any third party material used in this book and to comply with copyright law. Any queries in this respect should be brought to the attention of the publisher and any omissions will be corrected in future editions.

A CIP catalogue record for this book is available from the British Library.

Paperback ISBN: 9781036701581

The EU GPSR authorised representative is Logos Europe, 9 rue Nicolas Poussion, 17000 La Rochelle, France

contact@logoseurope.eu

Chapter One

Flames surged into the midnight sky as Kayden and Rosalyn escaped to freedom on their stolen horse. Its hoof beats thundered on the turf and in the moonlight, the animal's laboured breathing streamed past them in a frosty cloud.

Lying low along the gelding's back, both Kayden and Rosalyn urged him to go faster, while sparks drifted to the ground around them like dying fireflies. Having no saddle or bridle, they gripped the animal with their legs, and clung to his heaving sides as he streaked across the grass, a weakening Kayden holding tight to Rosalyn's waist.

Behind them, the great timbers of the catapult snapped and crackled in the consuming fire they had risked their lives to light. An amber glow flickered against the thick forest wall ahead. Concealment was close, yet Kayden knew Commander Adlard and the rest of Respiele's army would be organizing. It wouldn't be long before Kayden and Rosalyn were pursued in retaliation for their deeds. Particularly when Adlard discovered the Emerald was missing.

Respiele, leader of this enemy camp, would not be pleased to learn the weapon he planned to use to destroy Larkender Castle, had been burnt to ashes by mere children. Kayden could hear Adlard hollering in the distance. Heads would roll. Silently, Kayden willed their horse to run like the wind, because he carried the Emerald—lost jewel of the four Gems of Power. The Emerald alone held the power to heal Erinbourne, the alternate universe to Kayden's own. The Emerald was the only reason he and Rosalyn had been taken.

But after escaping, Kayden and Rosalyn had eluded Respiele's men of war, thus far, and they had a head start. The precious Emerald must be delivered to King Larkender before it was too late. Erinbourne was in danger of being overthrown by Respiele, the king's brother and enemy. The castle, and the king for whom Kayden carried the gem, were already under siege somewhere to the north.

They plunged into the woodland, Kayden clinging to Rosalyn, his breath coming in short gasps of pain. For a girl he had only just met in the heat of battle the day before and knew virtually nothing about—apart from her amazing ability to use a sword—she had become his most important ally. He swayed from dizziness behind her, nearly toppling to the ground. The throbbing ache in his shoulder where Adlard's sword had pierced him, coupled with a loss of blood from the wound, left Kayden faint. In his thoughts, he reached out to the Emerald for healing power—and the gemstone rewarded him with a hum of energy.

A consuming warmth seeped along Kayden's leg where the jewel lay in his pants' pocket. The Emerald's healing spread up his torso like curative fingers until it found the enflamed shoulder, numbing the pain as it explored the wound to heal Kayden's flesh. He felt the prickling heat as the energy coursed through his body. Then, as the Emerald sealed the gash shut, it grew cool against his thigh once more. A sigh escaped Kayden's lips and the gem became still.

Their horse slowed to a walk. The brush was thick, forcing the animal to push its way through the dense under-growth. Branches tangled in Kayden's hair, scraped at his jean-clad legs and jacket, and plucked like greedy fingers at Rosalyn's long cloak, threatening to pull them off the horse's broad back. Somehow helping one another, they managed to stay seated and continue to move ahead.

Despite the crashing noise of their progress through the thicket, the shouts and pounding hooves of their pursuers rose loud into the night. Kayden's stomach knotted, yet he knew that if *their* horse had to slow down, so must the horses and men behind them.

A light rain began to fall. Bad weather pushed in from a sharp wind that whistled in their ears, caused the clouds that had threatened all evening to finally give up their moisture. He and Rosalyn drew their cloaks tighter against the cold needles of water, closed their eyes, and let the horse pick his path. Then, remarkably, they were free of the brush.

With her face buried in the horse's mane, Rosalyn ran a hand along their steed's wet neck and spoke softly to him. Her words were ripped away by the wind, but the horse flicked his ears back and forth to listen. Somehow he had heard her. Changing direction, he burst into a tireless gallop across the open meadow they had entered, before lunging into another stand of timber.

Rosalyn reached back and pulled at Kayden's sleeve to get his attention. He inclined his head. Craning her neck and placing her lips so close that her breath tickled his ear,

Rosalyn whispered, "There is a Resistance base some distance ahead. The horse will take us." Readjusting the sword, where it hung from her belt and bounced along the length of her leather-clad leg, she stretched forward over the horse's neck to offer encouragement into his pricked ears.

Kayden nodded, even though she couldn't see him. "Guess it's a good thing I learned how to ride," he mumbled to himself. Gratitude rushed over him as he thought of all the time he'd spent at the family ranch on horseback. One or the other of his grandparents had ridden daily through the pastures to check the large herds of Charolais cattle they raised, and they had always taken him along.

He wondered what was happening with his family right now. It was easy to imagine them sleeping in their cozy beds on such a night. Maybe Gran was already out of the hospital. Then, remembering what Durgot had said about the passage of time from one land to another, Kayden thought perhaps nothing at all had happened since he'd left. And yet, so much had changed for him. He wasn't the same person.

He and Rosalyn rode into the night, winding their way through dense areas of the strange trees Kayden had grown accustomed to, as well as tall stands of pine. The pines were not so harsh on their bodies to push through. Sticky, but their sharp, pungent scent was almost comforting, reminding him of the ranch back home.

Then they were into the thickets again where grasping branches scratched their hands and faces till they drew blood and tore the hair right from their heads. Yet neither Kayden nor Rosalyn made a sound. The noises behind them were indistinct now.

Had they lost their pursuers?

However, with the pattering of the rain and their own

loud passage through the trees, it was hard to be sure. It wasn't safe to make any more noise than necessary. Then, only a few moments later, Kayden heard the long, haunting howls of the hounds that he had met the night before with the hedgehog, Talbot. The beasts seemed to be calling to one another. Thankfully the howling sounded far away, but it was both to the left and right of them. The hounds were closing in and leading Respiele's men straight to them with their plaintive cries. Rosalyn felt for Kayden's hand and clutched it tight.

The race was on.

Beneath Kayden's legs, the horse tensed and moved forward with a new urgency, but Kayden sensed that out of fear, the animal had lost its sense of direction. The horse moved randomly one way and then the other as the baying hounds came closer.

Kayden tapped Rosalyn's arm, leaned as close to her ear as possible, and murmured, "Maybe you should communicate with the horse again? I think he's scared, and with this rain and the darkness, he's off course."

He felt her nod in agreement.

Rummaging around in his pocket wasn't easy, since his pants stuck to his body like a dripping, second skin. Finally, Kayden located the boussole Durgot had given him, the small triangular object that was both compass and light. He pulled it out with a sharp exhale of breath. The rain had slowed to a drizzle, but their horse had slowed too. Finally, he came to a halt, tossing his head.

Kayden brushed a hand across his eyes to clear away the drips of water running down his face. There was no time to waste. He didn't even know if what he was going to try would work.

Flipping the boussole open, he tried to clear his mind of

the rising panic in his heart and bend his mind to the task. A soft golden glow lit up his hands and the rough brown cloth of Rosalyn's cloak as he peered down at the flashing silver object. Each hand on the sequence of dials spun alarmingly out of control. Kayden took a deep breath and steadied himself.

The yapping grew closer. One lone howl split the air. Then, the entire pack began to bay. Clearly, Respiele's emissaries had found the trail they were searching for. It was only a matter of minutes before the pack of hounds found Rosalyn and him.

Kayden narrowed his eyes and concentrated, willing the boussole to respond to his silent query. *Which way to the Resistance camp?*

The frenetic spinning of the boussole's dials ceased and the hands inside it pointed. A beam of light shone sideways from the boussole. It was pale, but it was enough. Rosalyn urged the horse along the wavering path.

The gelding cantered through the forest, weaving through the trees with remarkable agility. Kayden held the boussole steady, but glanced behind them every few seconds. Any moment, he expected to see pinpoints of light appear in the darkness, signalling the arrival of the Hounds of Enfer. Yet, he knew the horse they were riding had travelled as quickly as had been possible through the seemingly endless labyrinth of trees.

Without warning, Kayden, Rosalyn, and their horse burst from the treeline. In the thread of golden light from the boussole, Kayden could see they were caught in a channel between two sheer walls of rock that hemmed them in on either side. Their horse didn't miss a stride. Without the hindrance of trees, the animal doubled its pace, hurtling them along the passage with amazing speed as it leapt over fallen rocks and debris that littered the narrow path.

"Do you recognize this place?" Kayden yelled into the wind. There was no reason to keep silent now since their trail had been found.

"Yes. It is the right way," Rosalyn said. Yet, Kayden could tell she was worried. She shoved her sodden cloak away from her leg and rested a hand on the hilt of her sword. "I do not believe we can outrun them, Kayden, but we shall not go down without a fight."

The gelding whinnied in terror as his keen hearing picked up sounds of the hounds closing in behind him.

Behind them, the scraggly grey shapes of the hounds scrambled and skittered among the rocks at the mouth of the passageway, their long claws sliding along the granite for a foothold in their frenzied rush. The howling increased in volume. It was a cacophony of sound, echoing up and along the mountainside. The gelding tore around a curve and out into an open area at full speed, straining every muscle to stay ahead of the terrifying hounds.

Rosalyn and Kayden were thrown forward, nearly pitching headfirst into the jagged rocks that covered the path as their mount skidded to a halt, his sides heaving as he took in great gulps of air. Kayden squinted through the gloom. They stood at the base of a recent rockslide. Rocks were still tumbling down to land at their feet while a rubble of boulders and fragments of sheared off trees appeared in the flickering light of the raised boussole. Clouds of dust filled the air, making it hard to breathe. Petrified, Kayden held his boussole higher, frantically scanning the rocks for a way around or over the mass of rock.

There was none.

Turning, Kayden and Rosalyn faced the onslaught that

rounded the last bend and slid to a stop in front of them. The gelding threw its head and snorted, twisting first one way and then the other in terror. It struggled to face the hounds head on and protect its flanks. Red eyes glowed like tiny bobbing lights as the wolfish animals slowly, almost leisurely, padded toward Kayden and Rosalyn on the heaving horse. There seemed to be hundreds of the glowing orbs. Low growling ricocheted off the rock, filling the enclosed space beneath the mountain with menacing tones.

"If you can escape and find your way to the Resistance —leave me, and go," Rosalyn hissed from the corner of her mouth. She slid from the back of the exhausted horse, moved forward to face the hounds, spread her feet wide apart, and lifted her sword.

The first rosy light of dawn edged over the rocks high above the imminent battle and filtered down the path from where they'd just come. Kayden gazed at Rosalyn as he slid himself forward along the back of their horse and wound his hands into the animal's mane. He felt amazement for this fearless girl who was prepared to sacrifice herself for him and for the Gemstone of Power he carried. But there was no way she could hold off these horrible creatures. He must help her. *Why didn't I bring the Runestaff?*

Furious with himself, he shone his boussole back along the passage where they'd just been. Dozens of eyes gleamed back at him. They had ceased to advance, however. They waited for Respiele's men, swiftly coming up behind them on horseback.

With a clatter of horseshoes on stone, the enemy riders appeared. One by one, the hazy figures filed along the passageway and entered the canyon. There was no need to hurry, now. Kayden and Rosalyn were caught in a trap they could not avoid.

Kayden counted ten riders. They filled the small space cleft out at the base of the mountains and their mood of victory was palpable. He could hear the metallic twang of their swords being unsheathed as they came to a halt.

Kayden's horse whinnied with fear. Stamping its hooves and swinging its head from side to side, the horse was clearly weighing its chances of galloping down the passage to safety. Kayden did his best to soothe the animal by leaning forward and stroking its neck while keeping a close eye on what was happening. Movement caught his eye. Looking to either side of the canyon, he saw several of the hounds could not contain their thirst for blood. They picked their way along either side of the rockslide. Their large paws making no sound with the fallen rocks and dim light covering their movements..

Kayden silently awaited his doom, his eyes darting about the company of enemies who stood before him.

Who would make the first move?

The hound closest to Kayden snarled, his lips peeled back to reveal jagged teeth. Crouching low, he sprang. The animal's heavy body knocked Kayden flying from the horse. He and the hound bowled over and over painfully on the sharp rocks.

Kayden's horse reared and shied away, neighing, but the hounds weren't interested in a horse. Rosalyn bounded to Kayden's aid. The enormous hound sank its slavering jaws into the bulky material of Kayden's coat and flung him to and fro like a rag doll. While others, baying with excitement, raced to join the fray.

Kayden punched the huge bony head of the hound with all his might, but his blows bounced off the hard skull and left his fist throbbing with pain. He tried to twist himself from the animal's grasp and kick, but its jaws were locked, and its mind was set to kill.

Kayden's head banged on the rocks. Stars floated between him and the hound. Yet rising above it all, Rosalyn swam before his eyes. With one fluid movement, she thrust her shining sword into the hound's side and then yanked it free. There was a yelp and the thing went limp, its jaws falling slack. It sank on top of Kayden, pinning him down. With effort he pushed the hound off, blinking to clear the fog of concussion.

Rosalyn slashed at the hairy bodies around them. She towered over Kayden, ducking to avoid the frantic, lunging attacks of the creatures, and laying open every hide that came in reach. Thus far she had been successful, but it couldn't last for long. The riders were moving.

"Get up!" Rosalyn panted, plunging her sword down through a hairy skull with a sickening crunch. "Climb the rocks to—"

She was cut off by a long, low whistle from one of the men sitting astride a horse. Every hound that was able, slunk away as the warrior lifted his bow and trained it on Rosalyn.

"Give yourself up, boy, or I shall loose my arrow upon your friend." The warrior's ominous words rattled around the enclosed space. One of them had moved closer. He drew the string back to his shoulder and waited.

Rosalyn stood defiantly over the carcasses of several fallen hounds. "Do not do it," she said in a husky voice.

Kayden pulled himself to his knees and then stood, reeling. The sky was lighter now and much of the dust had settled. Shafts of sunlight streaked across the tumbled boulders where the path to safety had so recently been. Kayden's heart sank in defeat.

Then, yet another noise captured his attention. A few tiny pebbles bounced down the heap of loose stones. Was there going to be another slide? This time burying them all? Kayden lifted a hand to massage his throbbing head. All eyes turned to the rockslide as it glowed in the hazy red light of dawn. The rocks appeared to be moving. Kayden rubbed his eyes, forgetting for a moment, the terror that was behind him. He was completely in wonder of the brown shapeless lumps tumbling toward him from down the mountainside.

We should move or we're going to be crushed, he thought dully. But there was no sound of rocks crashing into rocks. Apart from the trickling clatter of smaller stones rolling down the hill, the shapes were soundless and impossible to make out as they trundled toward the tense assembly on the canyon floor. Only the sounds of horses stamping and shuffling, a low growl of the hounds, and the clanking of weapons from the enemy riders could be heard.

Then, the rider who had spoken screamed a warning. "Take the boy and get back down the passage." Two men leapt to obey. They flung themselves from their saddles and raced toward Kayden. But they were too late. Kayden squinted against the advancing light to see that it was not rocks, but living beings that hurtled down the uneven mountainside. Even as the riders tried to snatch Kayden and escape, the creatures launched themselves into the air and attacked. They were people of all sizes, dressed in long, brown, shapeless clothes that masked their identities.

Rosalyn whooped for joy and yelled, "The Resistance is here."

Chapter Two

The people of the Resistance swept over Kayden like an ocean wave—relentless and strong. Men and women brandishing crude weapons, leaped from stone to stone as they flooded down the rockslide and engulfed Respiele's army. The Resistance wore no armor, and one fell as a whistling arrow met its mark, but they were an unstoppable force. The light of the rising sun rose behind them, baptizing their purpose with its blessing. The fight was over in a matter of moments.

Many of the hounds, yelping in fear, scrambled down the passageway and escaped, but Respiele's soldiers were quickly surrounded and subdued. A tall woman with jet black hair woven into a long braid, gave orders that the wounded Resistance fighter, the prisoners, and their horses be taken the long way round, back down the passage and to the base a different way.

As the group filed around the winding corridor and out of sight, she rounded on her heel and strode to where

Kayden was sitting on a fallen pine tree at the foot of the slide, holding his head in hands that rested on his knees.

"Be ye well?" she questioned with a furrowed brow.

Kayden looked up briefly with half closed eyes and lifted a hand with thumb extended up to show that he was.

"This means yes?" she asked in a slightly puzzled tone that only Kayden could hear. When he nodded, she crouched down to add more gently, "And the gem?"

"It's fine," Kayden said, wondering how she knew he had it. Tentatively, he touched the right side of his head above the ear. It was wet and his hair was matted and sticky. He looked at his hand. Blood.

His first thought was of the Emerald in his pocket and the healing power it possessed. He felt it respond. His thoughts having figuratively, flipped on the switch to activate it. Except when the woman before him stiffened, he schooled his thoughts back to focus on the pain.

Perhaps these people could feel the presence of the Emerald, especially if it was at work. He remembered how Durgot had cautioned him against even showing it to anyone, let alone using it in front of them.

"Good," she said. She smiled at Kayden with a flash of crooked teeth. "I am Sonalia, leader of this group of Resistance fighters. Talbot told us to expect you and him both, and to aid in your journey wherever possible, but..." She paused to glance around, as if only noticing his absence now. "Where is Talbot?"

"I left him in Norbern," Kayden answered with effort. "Not intentionally, of course, but it *was* my fault. I tried to help with something and only made a mess of it."

He subsided into silence again, staring at the ground.

"There will be time to explain later," the woman said curtly. "We must make our way across the rock and back to a place of safety without delay. You will be in need of sleep and nourishment."

Raising an arm, she beckoned to one of the brown-clad men who stood nearby. "Maleson, see that you accompany this young man for the trip back, and fetch him and Rosalyn a flask of water. They must be thirsty."

Maleson hurried over, extending a flask he pulled from a strap on his side. Kayden reached for it and drank deeply.

"Thank you." He handed the flask back and watched as the man bustled over to where Rosalyn spoke with a few of their rescuers, seeming to know them well. She accepted the same flask and her eyes met Kayden's as she drank. Wiping her mouth on a sleeve, Rosalyn handed it back and strode over to him.

Kayden made no effort to move, other than to cradle his head in his hands. The throbbing pain from the first blow he had received back in the town of Norbern, where he had run into Adlard and been captured, had returned after being thrown onto the rocks by the huge hound. He was finding it difficult to see clearly.

"Are you able to walk?" Rosalyn asked, her voice filled with concern. "The camp is not too far from here. I've spent the last several years there, training for battle." She paused. "I know your head has been injured, but I would not use the Emerald for healing here if I were you. It is a powerful force that can be felt by those who know it. Wait until we are alone."

Silently, Kayden agreed, glad he had read the situation right for once. He reached out a hand to gratefully accept Rosalyn's help to rise. With the others, they began the long, arduous climb up and over the rockslide and down the other side. A few followed in their wake to assure they were not attacked from behind, but the Resistance were light-footed and sure, making short work of the difficult climb. Kayden struggled to keep up.

After laboriously reaching the same narrow passageway, found on the other side of the rockslide, they wound their way down it at a brisk pace. From there, they left the security of the solid rock walls and dove into a thick pine forest. Kayden was staggering quite a bit by this time and only opened his eyes occasionally. The aching in his temples was affecting his balance and he pitched forward, only to be caught by the strong hands of Maleson.

"Never fear, lad, I have ye," Maleson said in a deep fatherly voice. He patted Kayden on the back and then slid his hand under Kayden's arm for the remainder of their journey. The group walked two abreast along a worn dirt path through the woods.

Fingers of light and warmth stole through the thick pines above and with the sunshine, Kayden's spirits lifted a little. They were safe, at least for the time being. Thanks to Maleson's guidance he had allowed himself to be blindly led to wherever it was they were going, but now he lifted his head and picked up his dragging feet.

"We be almost there, lad," Maleson said.

Tentatively, Kayden opened his eyes a crack and peered about him. The group marched both in front and behind him, their footsteps barely making a sound on the path. A bird trilled nearby and in the underbrush close at hand, an animal rustled through the leaves as it went about its business.

Kayden wasn't sure where Rosalyn was yet could feel that she was close. He turned to look deep into the shadowy woods to his right. A strange flash of white, almost like a massive set of wings, caught his eye as it dove high into the branches of a tree. He wondered what it was. Maybe another outlandish creature that lived in this place or some sort of large bird? They moved past it, and he closed his eyes again. It had cost him dearly to keep them open for so long.

One minute they were walking in the deep undergrowth of the pine forest and the next they stepped into a clearing surrounded by the densely growing woodland. So dense, Kayden thought. Taking a chance at further pain, he gazed around him. It was as if it was bordered by a thick pole fence, impossible to push through.

Along the far northeast side stood two long timber buildings. From one, a thin stream of dark smoke puffed into the air. A large paddock filled the area to the west, made of the straight and sturdy timbers that stoically guarded them. Horses stood within the walls with tails swishing against the ever-present flies, relaxed, and resting. Between that area and the buildings were several sheds and huge stacks of hay. At the center was a spindly tower that soared high above the trees. At its top was a small, covered hut which must be a lookout point.

He held a hand to his brow. He had to find a place to disappear to, so he could summon the power of the Emerald to heal his aching head. It was hard to even open his eyes, let alone think about his next move.

The group moved across the open area and Kayden stumbled beside Maleson toward the building with the smoke curling from its roof. Sonalia disappeared within as each one behind her did in turn.

It was dark inside. Kayden opened his eyes enough to see that the only light came from small windows along one side. Maleson guided him to a roughly constructed chair that hunched at the end of a long dining table made from rough planks, and gently pushed him down to sit. The tantalizing aroma of food cooking over a fire wafted through the air so tangibly that Kayden felt he could reach out and grab it. He was starving.

Maleson stooped to speak directly to Kayden. "Before we commence eating, I shall be attendin' your wound, lad. Wait here."

He shuffled toward what looked like the kitchen. Rosalyn plopped onto the seat beside Kayden.

"Tell him you need to relieve yourself," she whispered into his ear. "There's a small shed around back. No one will follow you and you can call upon the…"

"Okay," Kayden jumped in, before she felt the need to explain further. "I get it."

Kayden waited until Maleson returned with a basin of steaming water and a length of clean cloth. The man set them on the polished boards of the table and motioned for Kayden to turn his head. Kayden held up a hand.

"Sorry," he said with a grimace suggesting an urgent need. "May I use the toilet first?"

"Aye, lad, there be an outhouse near the woods behind the far dwelling," Maleson said. "But hurry yerself back. That wound needs attendin' and breakfast be ready."

Kayden stretched his lips into a smile, stood up, and turned to push his way past a crowd of people talking by the doorway. They stopped their chatter to peer at him curiously. As two men moved to stop him, Kayden caught Rosalyn's eye and raised his brows. *Help.*

Ever so slightly she nodded, before leaping to her feet with a blood-curdling scream. She pointed a trembling finger at the floor beneath her seat. The whole place went still as people craned their necks to see what was the matter.

"A mouse!" she screeched. "I…I saw a mouse."

Kayden chuckled to himself as he scurried out the door

unnoticed. As if the Rosalyn he was beginning to know, would be afraid of such an insignificant thing as a mouse. With one hand on his forehead and the other trailing along the side of the house for support, he made his way to the squat little building near the tangle of brush at the forests edge and pushed open the door.

It didn't smell great, but at least he had privacy. Reaching a hand into his pocket he felt the cool, smooth sides of the Emerald. He turned his thoughts to it, and the Emerald flamed to pulsating life. A green glow spread from Kayden's pocket to fill the small dank, smelly space, and the medicinal waves of heat washed over Kayden, bathing him in its healing light.

The pain in his temples receded until it was nothing but a memory. He felt his head. Nothing. The blood still plastered a matt of hair to his head, but all traces of the gash were gone.

"Thanks," Kayden said, patting the gemstone through his jeans.

Emerging from the outhouse, Kayden looked around him with interest now that his vision had returned to normal. The grass beneath his feet was lush and green, but cropped short by a couple of horses that were hobbled nearby, and chickens pecked contentedly underfoot. Nearby there were two other pens—one with a few cows lying lazily in the sun to chew their cuds, and another with a low shed built at one end that housed an assortment of pigs. Kayden wrinkled his nose and kept walking. The Resistance had a good thing going here. They appeared self-sufficient and strong.

Past the pigs, Kayden breathed deeply. It felt so good to be pain free. The scent of pine and clean mountain air filled his lungs, reminding him of camping trips he'd taken with his parents. At this moment, life was good.

He had just rounded the corner of the dining hall when a flash of white, arching through the sky, caused him to stop. There it was again! Shielding his eyes against the late morning sun, he tried to see the thing, but it was gone.

Entering the hall, he moved to one side and shrank along the wall so as not to attract more attention. His face was unfamiliar to these people and his clothes were so unlike theirs that he stood out. While he felt safe, knowing they were all fighting for the same cause, he wanted to avoid any questions as to who he was or why he was here.

In the light that slanted through the few open windows in the south wall, he spotted Rosalyn still seated where he'd left her. The whole room was eating by this time, and few were talking, or looking around. Head down, he made his way down the length of her table and leaped over the bench to seat himself across from her. There was a dish of steaming food waiting for him and he tucked into it. However, as he chewed, his eyes strayed over his plate to rest on Rosalyn. It was the first time he'd had a chance to really look at her.

He knew from before that she was somewhat taller than him, and slender, but he didn't know she was so pretty. She'd removed the hooded travelling cloak and her long dark hair swung forward, threatening to dip into her plate of eggs and toast, until she flipped it behind her with an irritated grunt. Thick lashes matched her hair and swept down to rest on fair cheeks as she chewed. She glanced up to catch him staring and smiled, her lips stretching over somewhat crooked teeth.

"Do I pass inspection?" she asked, her smile widening into a grin. Not waiting for a reply, she spooned the last of her hurried meal into her mouth and reached to add his dish to her own.

"You do not want these?" she asked, jerking her head to the sausages he'd left rolling across the tin plate. He shook his head. She grinned even broader before setting off to dump the plates on a table near the kitchen door.

Flushing with embarrassment, Kayden focussed on the spoon he still held in his hand. He hadn't meant for her to notice his unconscious inspection. Fortunately, no one else had observed it, especially since the food had been served. The tables in the great hall were filled with hungry people all chattering as they gobbled the tasty meal.

A chair next to Kayden creaked as Maleson lowered himself onto it with his basin of water and cloth.

"That noggin of yours needs tendin' to," Maleson said.

Kayden turned obligingly as Maleson wrung out the cloth and began to clean away the blood.

"Sonalia wishes to see you and Rosalyn. After you finish eatin' of course. And she asked me to find you some other clothes." He pulled back to eye Kayden's garb with a frown. "You stick out like a five-legged dog!"

Kayden smiled. He was glad the Resistance leader of this group had thought of getting him something else to wear.

"You were lucky," Maleson said, tossing the cloth into the basin and getting to his feet. "I cannot find any wound at all on your head. Must 'ave been the blood of one o' them hounds. How is the pain in your head?"

"I feel much better now. Thank you," Kayden replied.

Maleson put a hand on Kayden's shoulder and gripped him hard. "I shall find you later."

He pushed his chair back, picked up the basin, and headed down the hall in the opposite direction.

Rosalyn slid back into her place holding tin cups filled to the brim with water. "Drink up. We cannot loll about here. Sonalia is waiting."

Kayden gulped down the water and then stood.

"Your head is better?" she inquired, leading the way through the door and out of the busy hall. There were curious stares from the people they passed, but no one tried to stop him again.

Kayden nodded and breathed a sigh of relief as they walked across a grassy stretch toward the lookout tower. He was glad to be away from the throngs of people.

Rosalyn stopped at the base of the structure. "Naturally, I knew Respiele had stolen the Amethyst many years ago, but many thought the Emerald was lost. How came you to hold it?"

"It's a long story," Kayden said. "I don't understand most of it myself, but I will tell you later."

Nodding, she accepted his explanation and motioned up the tower. "Sonalia is up there. Are you alright with heights?"

Her bright blue eyes looked questioningly at him.

For an answer, Kayden put his foot on the lowest rung of the ladder and began pulling himself up the side. He still felt a little foolish for looking at her so admiringly earlier on.

It was a long climb, and high. Kayden had never been bothered by heights, and knew better than to look down, but he felt a little light-headed as they neared the top. However, knowing that Rosalyn was right on his heels kept him moving along at a brisk pace.

Finally, he stuck his head through the opening in the floorboards of the shelter, and then heaved himself inside where he sat on the floor panting a little, not from exhaustion, but from nerves. He wondered what Sonalia would say to him.

"Going down is worse," Rosalyn muttered, appearing behind him, then clapped her mouth shut as she saw Sonalia waiting for them.

Kayden and Rosalyn scrambled to their feet and straightened stiffly to attention. The mere presence of Sonalia commanded respect. She stood tall and erect beside a shorter man who gazed out over the side of the lookout with a silver spyglass in his hand.

"Excuse us, Malcolm," she said smoothly. "I must speak with these young people. We will meet again later."

The man inclined his head politely, snapped the spyglass shut, and handed it to Sonalia before walking over to the opening and disappearing down the ladder.

Sonalia stooped to slide a wooden cover over the gaping hole in the floor and then looked appraisingly at Kayden down a large, hooked nose. She was taller than Kayden remembered, probably six feet, and muscular. Yet she moved with a fluid grace. He had seen her fight Respiele's men last night and knew she was a formidable opponent.

"I am glad you are here, young Kayden, great-grandson of Respiele Larkender and heir to the throne of Erinbourne." Her eyes crinkled at the corners as she bestowed a slight smile on him before including Rosalyn in her welcome. "It is well our scouts became aware of your efforts to reach us last night or things may have ended quite differently."

Rosalyn had gone still after hearing Sonalia's greeting and Kayden knew she would have plenty of questions later.

Sonalia walked back to peer out across the forest to the west, beckoning them to follow. The small structure in which they stood was open to the air all the way around the top in a wide gap of about an arm's length. It began just under the eaves, allowing the sentry to see in any direction without being exposed to the elements. Below this gap, all the way round, ran a narrow shelf. Where they stood, the shelf held a tightly rolled scroll, a few thick papers, and an assortment of rocks. A long, sharpened feather lay beside a metal container of what Kayden supposed must be ink. There were two uncomfortable looking chairs, and a long ivory colored horn hung from a wooden peg on the wall, attached at both ends by a length of leather.

"Look there." She pointed far into the southwest where a faint, pointed ridge of mountains could be seen poking over the horizon. A bank of cloud, bordered in deep blue, hung low over the peaks. "Beneath that ugly cloud is Respiele's lair."

She sighed and handed Kayden the telescope. "At great expense of life and limb, our scouts keep track of his movements. As we speak, Respiele is making his way to Larkender Castle in the company of every deceived human and deluded creature he could summon to fight for his cause. Other troops, such as the ones you ran into, will join forces with him there and they will attack as soon as possible."

Kayden extended the spyglass, put it to his eye, and trained it in the direction she had shown. He gasped. Above the jagged mountain tops, which jutted into angry relief against the sky, the clouds were not hanging still as he had thought, but swirled furiously. They were a deep purple in color, edged with a boiling black rim that twisted and writhed in the light of day. Dark tentacles coiled down to the earth like the probing threads of a cancer seeking to infect the land.

He lowered the telescope and handed it to Rosalyn who

also held it to her eye. Sonalia met Kayden's worried gaze with her own.

"It is imperative that you reach the castle before Respiele," she said to Kayden. "King Larkender cannot stand against this evil without the might of the Emerald."

Rosalyn turned and lowered the spyglass. Her eyes looked huge and scared as she scanned the faces of both Kayden and Sonalia.

"Your paths are henceforth entwined," Sonalia addressed them both. "Fate has brought you together for its own purpose, and it is for the good of us all."

She smiled again and grasping each of their shoulders she squeezed reassuringly.

"I can supply you with a horse to take you as far as possible along the route I will show you," she said, "but after that you must climb the mountains yourself and find Honistel Pass. It is the quickest route to the lower half of the River Glee and the closest and safest bridge to Larkender Castle."

Kayden and Rosalyn exchanged glances.

"I am sorry your way from here is so hard, but following the road would take longer and be much more treacherous now. It is not safe to travel in the lowlands at all. Respiele's men know where you are and what it is you carry. The Resistance members in our camp are not enough to withstand them, or to keep you and the Emerald from harm. Our path lies in a different direction. We must gather the other leaders and their Resistance groups to prepare for battle. As long as you and the Emerald are with us, our base is compromised…putting us all in grave danger."

She stepped to the back wall of the small hut and gestured to the north this time. "Those are the Maldone Mountains, and that is Mount Honistel. On the west side of it is the Honistel Pass. You need not know more names than that. It is your goal to cross over there. Neither Respiele, nor those who work in his service, will expect you take the hardest route. We will draw them off to the east while you make your departure…Up there." Sonalia pointed toward the distant peak.

She stepped to one side, so that Kayden and Rosalyn could have an unobstructed view of the imposing scene.

Kayden had to bend down in order to see up to the top of Honistel. It was the highest, snow-capped peak that he had *ever* seen; the almost sheer rock thrust up from the ground like an alien warhead.

"Mind you don't step on the trap door," Sonalia said, walking back to the shelf on the south end of the shelter. "Now, I want you both to look very carefully at this and commit it to memory."

She picked up the scroll and began to unfurl it using adjacent rocks to hold it flat. It was a crude, hand-drawn map.

She traced their route with her finger, showing them where to cross a stream, a gorge, and some landmarks to use in order to find the all-important Honistel Pass.

"Then," she went on, "you will have to pick your way down the other side watchfully, since Respiele's troops will be patrolling every inch of the River Glee on the other side.

"The River Glee flows from the far northeast of Tareele and splits into upper and lower Glee on its way to the Kalainian Sea. Upper Glee cuts beside a sheer mountain range making it impossible to reach the castle from any direction other than from the south, head on. Larkender Castle is on the north side of Upper Glee, built into the mountains."

"I have a boussole." Kayden's voice cracked a little.

Clearing his throat, he continued. "That should help with directions."

Sonalia arched her eyebrows. "Durgot's, I presume?"

Kayden nodded.

"Good, but it is better to have as much knowledge of what you are up against as possible. In any case, you must be tired," Sonalia said. She rolled up the map and stowed it under a ledge. "We will find somewhere for you to get some sleep and Maleson will prepare a travelling bag for each of you."

She flipped the trap door open with the toe of her boot and indicated that they descend. "You leave tonight under cover of darkness."

Kayden found that despite keeping his eyes firmly on the wooden ladder in front of him, his gaze was drawn to the foreboding Mount Honistel and the distance between where they were now and the gorge that marked the pass.

Some adventure, he thought a little bitterly. *We could be killed at any moment.*

Chapter Three

Kayden and Rosalyn hadn't spoken much after their meeting with Sonalia. The sight of Respiele's movements in the west, and the magnitude of what they had yet to do, were sobering for them both.

Once they reached the ground, Rosalyn pointed to the dining hall and told Kayden he would find Maleson inside. Then, she left, saying she would see him later. Kayden lifted a hand in farewell and walked back inside the long building to wait. Later, after he'd been given clothing and shown to his bed, he caught sight of Rosalyn out one of the narrow windows, first hugging, then talking animatedly with an older, silver-haired man near the horse paddock.

There was so much that Kayden didn't understand about this place and who these people were. Only his questions would have to wait for now. He was tired. Taking off his hiking boots and socks, he laid down upon the cot he'd been given and knew no more.

Kayden groaned. Someone was shaking him.

"I don't wanna go to school today." He rolled over to escape the hand that gripped his shoulder and then remembrance flooded his mind. He leaped from the hard cot, hitting the ice cold floor with his bare feet.

"Calm down," Rosalyn's voice whispered in the darkness. "It is I."

She held a candle in her other hand, the flame threatening to go out with all Kayden's activity. The glow cast eerie shadows across her features.

"You must get dressed and hurry. Maleson has prepared us something to eat before we leave."

She set the candle down on the table beside him and disappeared with a soft swish of her travelling cloak. Kayden took a deep breath and looked for the clothes he'd been given the evening before. They weren't as rough looking as the things he'd seen others wearing and he wondered why he'd been given the rich blue tunic, belted around the waist with soft leather. In any case, he dragged it on along with a pair of what Maleson had called breeches, and some tall, brown, well-worn boots. Picking up the candle and a heavy brown cloak much like Rosalyn's, he made his way to the lighted doorway of the kitchen.

"Come in," Maleson beckoned from behind a basin where he busied himself washing vegetables.

Kayden walked to where Rosalyn perched on a stool beside the hearth of a roaring fire. Maleson presented him with eggs, fried potatoes, and several thin slices of meat that Kayden figured must be venison. He found that he had no interest in the meat however, and pushed it to one side of his plate, noticing Rosalyn wasn't offered the meat. Something else to ponder.

"If ye are careful, ye have enough to eat for five days,

although you shall need to replenish yer water," Maleson said, breaking the strained silence that followed Kayden's arrival in the room. "Of course, it will not be takin' ye that long to reach the castle..."

He slung two identical brown bags to the floor beside them.

"I hope," he added quietly. He handed them each a heavy glass goblet with a small amount of steaming pink liquid swirling in the bottom.

Kayden looked at it dubiously.

"Drink up," Maleson said. "It be guaranteed to warm yer hearts and wake yer senses."

Kayden raised the goblet to his lips and took a sip. He spluttered, spitting half of it back out. "What is that stuff?"

"Mulled wine," Rosalyn answered dryly. "You have not tasted it before?"

"Oh. Sure. I've had lots of wine. Plenty of it," he lied, willing himself not to grimace as he took another swig. "It just—surprised me."

Thankfully, there was only a little of the rose-coloured liquid. He tipped it back, coughed once, and wiping his lips with the back of his hand, gave the goblet back.

"Thanks," he said to Maleson in a choked voice.

Picking up the bag, he shrugged the wide strap over his shoulders.

"Let's go," Rosalyn said.

They stole out the kitchen door and into the cold air that swept down from the mountain in a pine-scented breeze. Kayden had left his coat behind in order to complete his transformative look and had donned the warm woolen cloak he'd been given instead. He pulled it tight around him as he followed Rosalyn to the foot of the lookout tower where a shadowy figure awaited them with a horse.

Stars glittered brightly overhead, but the moon had become a thin shell of what it had been three nights before, offering only a vague separation between the ragged treeline and the night sky. An owl hooted somewhere in the distance. A hollow sound, underscoring the faint hope that Kayden felt, and he shivered despite the warmth of the wine that coursed through his veins.

Sonalia took a step toward them, passing the reins of the restless horse to Rosalyn.

"The Resistance will ride into the east tonight, as you begin the last, and most perilous, leg of your journey into the northwest," she said quietly. "Our departure will be noisy and large. With good fortune it will draw attention to us, and away from you. Godspeed to you both."

She reached for their hands and squeezed them tightly before melting into the night.

Kayden squinted after her before he noticed a group of people on horseback, milling in a tight circle near the treeline. With the muffled sound of hooves thudding on the turf, they were gone.

Rosalyn swung onto the horse's broad back wand reached a hand down to Kayden. Taking it, he sprang up and landed lightly behind her. She felt a close kinship with horses, he reminded himself, and was known by this group of Resistance fighters. She probably knew the terrain around here like the back of her hand. It was only right she should sit up front and guide the horse.

Nudging the animal with her heels, Rosalyn maneuvered their mount to the other side of the encampment. Then, without a backward glance, they pushed into the thick brush that lined the clearing and began the long, difficult climb to Honistel Pass.

Time passed slowly. They wound their way up through the thinning trees toward the dim spectre of the mountain ridge that hung dark and ominous above them. There were the usual night sounds: a scurrying of nocturnal animals in the underbrush, the swish of pines boughs swaying in a breeze that skimmed down from the mountain pass, and the sounds that they themselves made as the mare stepped on small branches and wound her way through springy shrubs.

For the first hour, they exchanged no words at all. It would have been unwise, after everything Sonalia had done to ensure they could exit the camp without being noticed, to risk alerting someone with the sound of their voices. But when they came to a wide gurgling stream, rushing down from the steep mountainside where the pine trees had loosened their grip, they stopped to discuss what should be done next.

"Sonalia told me this stream was not more than knee deep," Rosalyn said, pushing the hair away from her face. "We should be fine to cross."

Only the horse balked at stepping into the water. Rosalyn clucked and pushed the mare with her hands and legs, but it was to no avail. The horse snorted great clouds of steam and danced back and forth on the slippery bank, refusing to step into the water.

"Why don't you talk to her?" Kayden asked, leaning close.

"I have! It is not that simple. She does not want to go."

Kayden settled back, reaching out to their stubborn steed with his own questions.

Something smells wrong with this water.

To his great shock, the mare's response had floated into

his mind. Cool! He had doubted his ability, as one of the Garde, to speak with animals. After all, it had been a while since he'd done it with Talbot. A pleased smile flitted across his face. Gathering his thoughts, Kayden asked the mare if she would cross the water if he deemed it safe. She agreed.

"Rosalyn," Kayden said into her ear, "I'm going to get off and check out the stream myself."

She nodded and soundlessly, Kayden slipped to the earth. Rosalyn backed up the horse, giving Kayden room.

Reaching into a small pouch that had thoughtfully been included on his belt, he withdrew the boussole and opened it with a flick. The soft light from its interior was all he needed to spot some deadfall and he picked up a long, dead branch. Holding on to the boussole with one hand, he stepped to the water's edge and paused to aim the thin light of the boussole upstream.

It seems harmless enough, he thought. Perhaps he'd been dreaming to think a horse had spoken to him and moreover warned him about the babbling brook that gurgled past his toes. Hanging onto the branch by the widest end, he dangled it out over the stream and dipped its other end into the rushing water. Nothing happened. He shoved the stick deeper into the flow, to test the depth, and the silvery stream tugged it downstream, but there seemed to be no threats that he could perceive, and the water was shallow.

"It seems okay." He spoke not only to Rosalyn, but directed this information to the mare as well. Rosalyn was only a dim outline against the forest behind her, but Kayden saw her shoulders relax and she moved their horse forward again. Kayden swung up behind her.

The animal splashed into the stream, taking care with her footing on the slippery rocks beneath her hooves.

The moment she had all four feet submerged in the water; Kayden felt her stiffen.

Almost imperceptibly, the water rose. Swirling around the mare's fetlocks, it climbed faster, soon eddying about her knees and then her hocks, and with it came a heavy, drenching mist. Kayden didn't have to see it to know what the fog consisted of. He could feel the cold dampness and the dread that accompanied the fog that slid over his boots and sank into the thick material of his breeches as it sought to envelop them.

"Hurry!" He slapped a hand on the rump of the horse and felt the mare gather her strong hindquarters beneath her and lunge forward. With a ringing of metal horseshoes on rocks, she drove across the stream, pulling herself to dry land on the other side and shaking wildly to rid herself of the traitorous water.

"What was that?" Rosalyn demanded, once they'd righted themselves.

"That—was Respiele, or I guess a better way to put it, his weird spy. He uses a mauve-coloured fog to find the Emerald, but it's more dangerous than it sounds. It's mind-altering stuff. It gets into your head and infiltrates your brain with sick lies that make you feel like your worst fears are coming true.

"It travels well on water too," Kayden added bitterly, remembering his first encounter with the mist back in the hollowed out mountain when he'd first entered Erinbourne.

"Respiele has the Amethyst after all." Rosalyn shuddered. "No wonder the magic he uses is stained with its hue. It didn't have a chance to snare us in that brief space of time, but Respiele may know where we are headed from that encounter. We best get moving."

The incident, although unexpected and shocking, had

helped to dissolve any feelings of shyness between them and they began to talk in low undertones as the horse picked their way up a trail.

"So, you've never seen or experienced anything like that before?" Kayden asked. "It must float above the water everywhere in this—land," he finished awkwardly.

"No. But there are many things as cannot rightly be explained of late. Especially on this mountain. Sometimes, when I lived in the camp below, I would hear peculiar sounds and see odd lights up here."

"Great news," Kayden said sarcastically. He reached forward to push away a heavy branch as they both ducked under a scraggly tree. "So, now we have to deal with hauntings too. What's next? A zombie apocalypse?"

"What is a—zombie?" Rosalyn fumbled over the unfamiliar word.

"I was just joking," Kayden chuckled. "It's not real—at least, I hope it isn't, but in Erinbourne you never know."

His voice trailed off and then he picked up the conversation again.

"Why were you here, living with the Resistance?" he asked. "That was your father I saw in Norbern with the vegetables, right? Before we were captured?"

"Yes, that was him." She sighed. "I do hope he is safe."

She sank into her own thoughts and Kayden waited.

The breeze was cold, but invigorating, and pulling it into his lungs he breathed deeply. His senses felt alert. Had he ever felt this good back home?

"I was in Norbern that day to help my father, but I knew the Resistance was going to attack Respiele's army when they unloaded that weapon. I was there to fight with them," she said finally. "I have lived with the Resistance for two years. Ever since my mother died."

"Oh, I'm sorry Rosalyn." Kayden said. His brow furrowed. "That must have been really hard on you."

"It was. After she was gone, father and I decided I would join Sonalia and the Resistance group. My uncle—Uncle Eustace—trained me to fight. He has been here for many years, readying people for war. Everyone knew this day was coming and all those who could prepare for it, did."

"Well, from what I've seen, he trained you well, that's for sure. Do you suppose you could show me a few cool moves?" Kayden asked cheerfully, in an attempt to lighten her mood.

"I could teach you how to handle a sword, although it takes many years to be good at it, but I am not sure what a cold move is."

"A *cool* move," Kayden corrected with a chuckle. "It just means to do something that others would find impressive. Anyway, never mind," he finished, thinking the explanation sounded foolish, even to him.

"So, are you truly Respiele's great-grandson?" Rosalyn asked hesitantly, after a long while where they could only hear the sounds of the horse's hooves rustling through the pinecones and scraggly shrubs that grew among the trees.

"Yeah, that's what they tell me."

There was complete silence at this.

"I know. It's weird," Kayden answered with a shake of his head.

The whole thing was not only weird. It was embarrassing. He didn't want to reveal that the madman who was hunting them and bringing destruction and war to this land, was also his great-grandfather. Knowing she was waiting for him to continue he took a deep breath and went on.

"When Respiele fought with his brother, your King

Ludwig, he stole the Amethyst and took off on his own. Eventually Respiele ended up in the western mountain range. What's it called?"

"The Araleesh Mountains?" Rosalyn answered as if in a dream.

"Right. Well, Respiele chose a wife from the people of the Garde who lived there and together they had a girl called Alainea." Tonelessly, Kayden recited the information he'd been given by Durgot. "She's my grandmother."

"So, you are the grandson of Alainea." She stopped again and ran her fingers through her hair. "You really are Respiele's heir, and King Ludwig's also. Yes, that is very... *weird*, as you call it."

Rosalyn lifted both hands into the air, as if she were going to say something, then dropped them.

She giggled suddenly. "I suppose I should be calling you, 'Your Majesty'?"

"Maybe someday," Kayden agreed in a fake tone of grandeur, "but for now, Prince Kayden will do."

Rosalyn laughed, a light tinkling sound that warmed Kayden's heart. As they fell silent, he had a feeling they might be friends after all.

The night wore on. Despite the sleep he had managed the previous afternoon, Kayden began to yawn and his eyes felt heavy.

"Rosalyn? Wake up." Gently Kayden shook her slumping shoulders.

She jerked into wakefulness, her hand reaching for the hilt of her sword and her eyes wide and staring. The horse stood at the edge of the treeline. From here on out it was pure rock and far too steep for the faithful mare to continue.

"We have to send her back to the Resistance and walk from here," Kayden said. But before taking the next, inevitable step, they waited quietly in the dim shadows of morning, watching as the first shafts of light appeared behind them in the east.

Kayden slid to the ground and stretched. It had been hours since they left the camp. His back ached. Rosalyn jumped down beside him, unfastened the rope halter, and let it drop to the ground.

"It was not worth much and might well be hazardous to her safety if it were to catch in the trees," she said as Kayden's gaze followed the simple piece of equipment.

"Thank you," they chorused quietly, standing on either side of the mare to stroke her sleek neck. She nuzzled each one and then turning, started to pick her way back down the mountain slope the way they had come.

It was as Kayden watched the last swish of her tail disappearing into the evergreens far below that he noticed it —that same flash of white deep amid the shadows.

"Did you see that?" he asked worriedly.

"No, what?"

"I have this feeling that something is watching me, ever since the Resistance met up with us along that mountain pass." As he said it, he realized how crazy it sounded, and he hastened to tone down his concern. "Aww, it was probably nothing."

Rosalyn smiled. "I suppose a proper prince should have an entourage to protect him from such unknown entities."

Stuffing down his qualms, Kayden plastered a smile on his face. "I don't need an entourage. I have you."

They began to climb.

They were not so sure footed as their horse, but just as they reached a point where they needed light to be sure of their next steps, the sun began its lazy passage up into the eastern skies. A golden hue gilded the rocks, bathing the simple stones in a magical glow. Even Mount Honistel's jagged peaks softened slightly in the first rays of dawn.

"Thank goodness we don't have to climb over top of it," Kayden said. He felt a bit hopeless as he craned his neck back in order to see the very top. "I mean, it shouldn't be any problem at all to avoid Respiele's all-seeing sorcery, climb a mountain, skip around the side, find a secret passage—and watch out for a bunch of ghosts."

"We can do it." Rosalyn spoke forcefully, as though trying to convince them both. "We should try to find shelter among the rocks to rest for a couple of hours and eat something though. Perhaps up there."

She pointed. "It looks like a rocky overhang. Do you see it?"

Kayden nodded, and they struck out across the broken shale and stones at the base of Honistel where frequent rockslides had ground the lower parts of the mountain into pebbles. It was slippery going and they placed each foot carefully, not wanting to slide all the way back down and have to start again.

There was no talking now. They needed every bit of breath they had to work their way up to where the hulking rock, Rosalyn had spotted, lay in the midst of the rubble. Snatching at small shrubs and sturdy weeds for balance, they concentrated on moving their feet slowly and surely. The sun climbed higher. Finally, Rosalyn, who was ahead, raised a hand and then bent over double, panting.

"Just a few more steps, Kayden."

Kayden didn't reply. He paused, then together they continued to angle their way toward the rock.

Finally, Rosalyn dropped to her knees before the overhang and looked inside. Clearly satisfied, she crawled in on hands and knees, scrabbling her way under the huge slab and into the cool, dark recess. Kayden wasted no time in following her. They crunched over the cold grey stones, puffing with exertion.

Rosalyn had her sword slung over her back on a light cord, along with the bag that Maleson had thoughtfully packed with provisions. She sat up, dragged it off, and with effort, reached into the satchel to pull out a silver telescope, similar to the one Sonalia had used.

Kayden pulled himself to sit cross-legged beside her and busied himself with a flask of water. Rosalyn extended the lens and peered into the distance.

"I can see nothing following us," she said. Reaching for her own flask, she drank greedily before lifting the telescope to train it along the skyline further into the west. "Wait... There appears to be a large group of birds heading this way —crows I think, or maybe a huge flock of starlings." She studied them. "There are too many of them to be a natural occurrence though."

She snapped the telescope shut and slithered back as far as she could under the cover of the slab. Pulling her knees to her chest, she turned a face filled with fear to Kayden.

"Get back and be still," she hissed.

He did as she directed, holding his breath as the raucous cries and flapping wings of the birds rushed upon them, swooping and diving as they passed overhead. The flock filled the sky from horizon to horizon, as wide as the eye could see. However, not in the formation of an ordinary flock of birds, but as though they were a living carpet that flowed in an unending texture of pattern and shape. The number of small birds was so great that the sun could only peek fitfully through their mass as they flooded the sky with one mind, their sharp eyes leaving no crevice, nook, or cranny unexplored.

They were starlings, Kayden thought, but it was what appeared behind them that caused him to hold his breath in horror. Like a thread drawn into the eye of a needle and tugged through the fabric of the sky, a heaving ribbon of pure purple venom twisted and turned in the birds' wake. If the light and heat of the sun had disappeared, with the passing of the birds, it had vanished completely now.

The choking purple wave consumed the air. It curled and dipped, flooding over the rocky landscape and staining the trees where Kayden and Rosalyn had so recently been. It was an oppressive surge of color that snuffed out the day as effectively as if the sun itself had been extinguished.

It flowed close to the earth, but not flush with it. As it snaked across the land, Kayden shrank back, flattening himself into the broken rocks beneath him, hardly daring to breathe. Respiele's amethyst spy flowed over the slab above them. Somehow mercifully, it did not find them.

Closing his eyes, Kayden knew, beyond a shadow of a doubt, that the mist, the birds, and now the purple stain that saturated the sky, sought to find the Emerald—and to destroy the one who carried it.

Chapter Four

Kayden woke up later to find Rosalyn sitting cross-legged at the edge of their sanctuary, peering through her small silver scope. Earlier, they had decided through hand signals, to simply stay where they were until all traces of the birds and Respiele's purple smoke had passed. Then, as a consequence of lying so still and silent, sleep had claimed them both. Kayden wondered how it had been possible to rest in such stressful circumstances and on a bed of rocks. Yet he had dropped off almost immediately, as had Rosalyn.

Kayden pulled himself to a seated position with difficulty. Every part of his body ached. He rubbed his back where the jagged stones had become embedded in his skin.

"See anything?" he whispered.

"No."

"We should eat and then get going?"

Rosalyn nodded and slid herself back under the flat rock to join him in rummaging through their bags. They drew out the parcels of food that had been packed and laid them on their knees.

Weird, Kayden thought, as he unwrapped the food. Of course, he hadn't expected to find peanut butter sandwiches wrapped in plastic film and an Oh Henry chocolate bar. Despite that the hard brown bread and pale-yellow cheese, he did find looked strange in its oily cloth wrapping.

His eyes flitted up to meet Rosalyn's. She was laughing at him.

"Do you think it is perhaps, poison?" She snorted, tearing into her own crusty slab. "What do you usually eat?"

"Well, I eat bread too, it just looks a little different and we don't wrap it up in a greasy rag." Shifting his gaze back to the meal, Kayden lifted the slice tentatively to his mouth and took a tiny nibble. "Hey, it's good!"

He grinned at her.

It was hard, almost black in color, and more like a cracker than bread, but the flavor was rich, nutty, and delicious. He took a big bite and then tore off a piece of cheese and popped it into his mouth too. It was also firm, but melted in his mouth like warm butter.

They ate in a companionable silence.

"Your grandmother might be Garde, but you are not from around here, are you?" She asked it as a question, but it was a statement more than anything.

Kayden hesitated, not knowing how or what to tell her. "I'm not from Erinbourne at all."

Her eyes grew wide. "Please explain. And is this why you have the Emerald?" Rosalyn rested her elbow on a knee and propped her chin on her hand, prepared to listen.

"It's a really long story, and I don't know most of it." Kayden ran a distracted hand through his hair. "The truth is that I come from a world outside your own. Somehow, my grandmother met my grandfather here, in Erinbourne. He was from my side of the portal. Then, I guess they decided to get married and he took her back to live with him. She took the Emerald with her for safekeeping in my world. I didn't know anything about my heritage, or that Erinbourne even existed…until a few days ago when Durgot, the gate-keeper, found me. He asked me to find the Emerald and carry it to King Larkender. Without it, the king doesn't have a chance against Respiele."

"That is remarkable," she exclaimed. "I would like to hear all about it one day."

"So would I," Kayden said dryly. "That's pretty much all I know."

"The Emerald belongs on the king's sceptre," Rosalyn said, half to herself. "So does the Amethyst. With all four Gemstones the king has absolute authority over the land. With only two of them we are doomed…" Her voice trailed off at the end as though she were unwilling to put the grim prospect into words.

"Yeah, I know. That's why I'm trying so hard to get it to the king."

"My sword is at your service," she said formally and Kayden smiled.

"I myself am part Garde." Rosalyn shifted a stone out from under her leg. "My mother was from the north. The Tareele Mountains where King Larkender's castle lies. So, we are both part Garde and could both have communicated with the horse I stole," she mused. "I did not tell you I could speak to animals, because some Erinbournians misinterpret our abilities and distrust the Garde."

Kayden reached for his flask of water and nodded. "I'm kind of amazed that it's not a big deal for you to hear that I come from an alternate universe."

"I have known of the portals within the four mountain ranges in Erinbourne since I was a child and often wondered about the world beyond…your world." Rosalyn took another bite of food and chewed thoughtfully. "What is it like—where you live?"

She caught her hair behind her head and pulled it over one shoulder, her blue eyes studying Kayden's face.

"Well, I guess the landscape is similar to here, although we aren't surrounded by mountains on all sides. We grow crops too, and on the ranch, where I live, my grandparents raised cattle. My grandfather passed away a few years ago, but Gran kept the ranch going. The main difference between our lands is…" Kayden paused, unsure how to describe technology, industry, and transportation. "We're more—advanced."

"Advanced?" Her eyes narrowed. "Do you mean you are somehow better than us?"

"No. It's hard to explain. Instead of horses or wagons, we drive cars, or trucks, and we ride in airplanes when we have to fly long distance—"

She lifted a hand to interrupt him.

"You are telling me that you fly? Like a bird?"

"Well, we don't leap off a cliff, flap our arms, and zoom into the distance, if that's what you're asking." He smiled, hoping to elicit a similar response from her.

There was none.

"Now you mock me!" She lifted her chin and her eyes flashed as she waited for his response.

"No, no, please don't take offense! I'm not trying to mock you. It's just difficult to explain. A long time ago in my world, people invented something called a motor and then they built machines out of metal, like your sword is metal." He pointed to it for emphasis.

"A motor powers the machines or makes them move. Some of those machines are called cars. They're like wagons. We ride in them without needing a horse to pull us," he said, trying to make his explanation as simple as he could. "And then people figured out how to make enclosed wagons that could fly through the air with people inside."

Rosalyn stared at him like he was losing his mind.

"I am now concerned that the purple smoke has addled your brains," she said with genuine concern.

Kayden sighed and began to fold up the remainder of his lunch and stow it in his pack. It was too much to explain and for her to understand.

"Let's just drop it, alright?" he said. "Maybe someday I can show you in person."

Rosalyn shrugged. "In any case, it is time we continued our journey."

They eased themselves out from under the rock before standing up to stretch and rub aching muscles. The sun had shifted significantly and Kayden estimated it was about three o'clock. Thankfully, nothing moved either above or below them, and he relaxed a little. Rosalyn threw her pack over one arm and considered the sheathed sword in her hand before flipping the strap overtop her raven hair and adjusting it on her shoulder.

"When next we stop, I shall give you a short lesson in handling this." She gave her sword a pat and caught Kayden's eye. "If I were to be...Well, you ought to know something of how to defend yourself."

Together they twisted to look at the shining, snow-capped peaks of Mount Honistel.

"I think we should try to reach the very base of the mountain where we can find cover if those birds take another swoop through here. But we should aim toward the pass. What do you figure?" Kayden asked.

"Yes. We must get there before nightfall. It is not safe to walk the mountains at night."

The rocks were bigger now, and they stepped from one stone to another, aiming themselves on an angle toward the base of Honistel. Occasionally, a few rocks would dislodge and skitter down the steep slope beside them and they would stop, praying the sound would not alert anyone or anything to their presence on the mountainside.

However, all went well. Although progress was slow, they stood in the shadow of the towering giant in only a couple of hours. Huge boulders, having tumbled from far above somewhere in their prehistoric past, lay in their path. Craggy and imposing, they jutted haphazardly up the side of the mountain to where the pass lay. There was no need for the boussole just yet, since the direction to take was all too clear. Squaring their shoulders, they pressed on. This would be their greatest test thus far.

Under other circumstances this might have been fun, Kayden thought as he searched for a handhold on the smooth rock face he was climbing at the moment. However, he would have preferred being forced to wear a helmet and be strapped into safety equipment. There was nothing to save him in this situation. If he fell—he fell, tough luck.

There was a grunt from above, as Rosalyn disappeared over the top of the rock they'd been climbing. Then came the sound of scrabbling boots on rock. Kayden called to see if Rosalyn was alright just before hearing a frightened screech and a heavy thud. Telling himself not to rush lest he fall too, he hurried to the top of the rock as fast as he could make the climbing work: fit one foot into a cleft in the rock, pull up, reach for a handhold, and shift higher—repeat.

He reached the place where Rosalyn had been and crawled across the top of the rock to look down the other side. She lay on a wide ledge about five feet down into a chasm, her long black hair trailing over the rock and fluttering in a breeze that wafted from below.

Kayden caught his breath in great gulps, his eyes wide.

"Rosalyn!" His voice was high-pitched and hoarse.

"I am alright. Scared to death, but alright." Moving slowly, she pulled herself to a seated position and waited to catch her breath. Then she placed both palms flat on the ledge in order to safely stand.

"Ouch!" she cried, clutching her arm. She sat back down with a thump, her back to the rock wall. "I've broken my wrist."

He exhaled sharply.

"We can heal your wrist," he said, when he had calmed his voice enough to speak. "We just have to figure out how to get you out of there."

He sat back on his heels and looked around for inspiration.

"Kayden. I have a rope." Digging in her bag she pulled out a thin cord and tossed one end of it up to him with her good hand.

"Got it," he said, leaning over the edge to grab it as it snaked past his outstretched hand. "If you tie it securely around your waist, I'll pull you up."

"Alright," she called, a bit breathlessly. "I am ready."

Kayden wrapped the rope around each hand, braced his feet on rocks, and began to slowly haul Rosalyn up and over the steep overhang.

She collapsed onto the rock beside him, cradling her hand. Kayden extracted the precious gem from his pocket, eyeing Rosalyn's injury. Her wrist protruded at an odd angle and was swelling rapidly.

All color had drained from her face with the pain. But

she made no sound, even when the broken bones ground together as Kayden lifted her hand gently and placed the sparkling Emerald over top.

After asking what he needed from the healing stone, Kayden felt the familiar warming vibrations extend from the gem and radiate into Rosalyn. As the Emerald began to work, her eyes flew open wide. By the time the Emerald had cooled to the touch she was flexing her fingers experimentally.

"That is truly amazing," Rosalyn said in astonishment. Before Kayden knew what she was doing, she flung her arms around his neck to hug him close. "Thank you, Prince Kayden."

She released him with a happy smile.

Kayden felt his face flaming as hot as the Emerald had been a moment ago, and turning to hide his confusion, he made a fuss of coiling her rope and handing it to her.

"We'd better keep going," he mumbled. "But I think we should start looking for somewhere to camp for the night."

They picked their way along the ridge of rock where Rosalyn had fallen. They were well on their way up the lower left side of Mount Honistel despite the setbacks they'd faced that day. Nonetheless, shadows were lengthening against the face of the mountain and the sun would soon disappear behind the mountains, making their passage even more dangerous.

Ahead, Kayden could see what looked like a cave or crevice in the rock and he turned to point it out to Rosalyn.

"Approach it slowly, Kayden," she said. "It may be the home of some animal."

Considering the type of weird beasts Kayden had seen in this land already, he wasn't taking any chances, and fell back a step to wait for her.

"You know more about this than I do," he said. "Tell me what you think as we get closer."

They heaved themselves up onto a flat rock near the entrance to the cave and observed it doubtfully.

"I'm going to get closer and shine my boussole inside," Kayden said.

Gauging the distance, Kayden leaped from where they stood, to a rock just below the opening and pulled himself up to crouch in the mouth of the cave. He flipped open the silver boussole and beamed it inside.

"It *looks* fine," he called back to Rosalyn. "And don't see any signs of an animal, but I also don't have a good feeling about it. Appears to lead back into the mountain quite a distance too. Come check it out."

With a bound, she was beside him, peering into the dim recesses of the fissure.

"I think it's safe," she said, ducking inside.

The opening was not quite high enough for her to stand without her bending over, but grew marginally taller as they moved back into the cave, extending the boussole in front of them. It was a tiny space, a fracture in the rock running up into the stone above and tapering off back into the mountain behind them.

"I dunno," Kayden muttered. He moved back to the entrance and leaning a hand on the wall, he bent to look out at the setting sun. "I don't like it. I've watched enough movies to know that nothing good will come of staying in a place like this."

"I do not understand this 'movies,' word, but we can continue to look for a resting place if you would feel better about it," Rosalyn said. "However, we must hurry. Once the light is gone we will be forced to stop—wherever we may be."

"Naw, let's stay. We won't find anything better," Kayden said, running a hand through his hair so that it stood up on end like orange flames. He tugged the strap of his pack over his head and sank to the floor, as Rosalyn did the same. "I'll take the first watch. You get some rest."

With a grateful smile, Rosalyn lay down, curled up in her voluminous brown cloak, and went to sleep.

Later, when it was her turn, Kayden found he didn't have the heart to wake her. He stared into the velvety stillness of the night, listening to an owl hooting and the rustling of small nocturnal animals, and watched the first stars begin to glitter in a midnight sky. It seemed like he had sat hours with his arms clasped about his knees and his own cloak wrapped around him for warmth against the cold wind that gusted down from the icy peaks around them.

He had a lot to think about. Among other things, he contemplated his life so far...comparing the two places he knew and loved the best—the ranch, with its rolling hills, and bustling farm life, against his home in Toronto, the largest and, in his opinion, most exciting city in Canada. Was one better than the other? He didn't think so. Although, despite the anger that he'd felt for it only a few days before, Kayden knew he loved his life on the ranch the best.

The realization surprised him. He considered the friends he'd left behind in the city, the adventures he'd had growing up on the same street for fifteen years, and how upset he'd been to leave it all behind. Surprisingly, he found that thinking of it didn't upset him anymore.

Sure, he had some great memories and had done a lot of exciting stuff back then, but—he turned to look at the sleeping figure beside him on the rock—nothing could compare with this adventure. The only problem was he couldn't tell anyone. Or rather, they would never believe him if he tried.

Something inside him had changed, and he was glad. The Dillons of the world were insignificant in light of this knowledge. Smiling to himself, Kayden shuffled across the floor to lean his back against the wall of the cave and thought of Gramps, Gran, Mom, Dad, and—he grudgingly admitted—even Sarah. He missed them terribly. As the owl's mournful call once more echoed off Honistel Mountain, his eyes closed.

Something was wrong. Kayden's eyes flew open. He could hear a shuffling sound from the rear of the cave. Coming up onto his knees, he saw a light bobbing along the wall of the corridor leading back into the mountain and heard the unmistakable sound of something large being dragged.

"Rosalyn!" He pawed at the rock where she'd been, but there was nothing there now. He leapt to his feet as two hands grabbed him in the darkness. One went round his chest and the other forced a smelly rag over his nose. He struggled, elbowing his assailant in the ribs, and kicking at them, but he felt himself getting woozy and weak.

Everything went black.

Chapter Five

Kayden woke up first. His hands and feet were bound. Though his vision was blurry, he could see that he lay on a wooden floor, looking at the wall of what appeared to be an old log cabin. He licked his lips. His mouth felt like dust. Behind him came a moan and he knew it was Rosalyn.

What had happened? One minute he was coming to some major conclusions in his life, and the next he was attacked by some unseen hands and dragged into that stupid cave. Although he ached all over, Kayden thrust out with his feet. Pushing himself around, bit by bit, he was able to look into the room. They appeared to be alone. A fire burned brightly on the other side of a coarsely made table. Several chairs were shoved beneath it. From one hung two dead rabbits, snared and their feet bound together with cord. In the corner was more home-made furniture: a wide bed, covered in assorted filthy cloths, a rocking chair, and another, smaller table that held a wash basin and pitcher.

"Oh, deary dear! Here he comes," said a high, squeaky voice. "And I hasn't got any vittles cookin'."

Guess we aren't alone, Kayden thought. His heart raced and he felt panic building in his chest. His body grew hot and his limbs went weak. He didn't have a clue how they could escape, or how he could protect the Emerald. Kayden shut his eyes, leaving one open just a crack, hoping that whoever was talking might reveal something important while believing he was unconscious.

A door slammed, the force of it rattling dishes somewhere Kayden couldn't see.

"Woman! Did ye check them for valuables?" an angry voice boomed.

"What did ye say?" asked the whiny voice.

"Did ye find any money on 'em?" the angry voice bellered, slowly and distinctly. "I went through the bags twice, but there was nothin'. Look in their pockets."

There was a scrambling noise as someone scuttled around the table. They dropped to the floor and frantically began rifling through Rosalyn's pockets. She groaned and Kayden barely suppressed an angry demand that their captors leave his friend alone. But nothing he could do would change what was happening now. It was one more situation where he blamed himself for losing the Runestaff.

"Nothin'," the whiny voice announced before shuffling over to Kayden.

Claw-like hands rolled him over and he felt fumbling fingers digging through his pockets. He stiffened and held his breath, instinctively drawing his legs up to protect the enchanted Emerald. This was awful.

"I got sumpthin!" the woman yelled in triumph.

Heavy footsteps clumped over to stand beside Kayden's head.

The pouch Kayden had been given at the camp, in

which to house the Emerald, was yanked from its hiding place in the front pocket of his breeches.

"Give it over!" the man barked. "Be it money?"

Kayden heard a smack and a yelp, as the man's hand met with some part of the woman's body, and she fell to the floor at Kayden's feet. The man threw himself into one of the chairs.

Risking detection, Kayden slowly tilted his head and looked at his seated captor. The man was huge. He sprawled over the tabletop, fingering the finely woven material that held the Emerald. His face was tanned brown as a walnut from hours in the sun, and he had a white fur hat yanked low on his head. His lips were thin and compressed in a cruel line, and his eyes glinted with anger and greed. A long scar ran down one cheek, although it was hard to see for all the long, greasy, grey hair that fell across his face from under the hat.

Kayden had seen enough and closed his eyes. This was terrible. Yet, somehow he couldn't help himself and opened them a crack once more.

Weighing the sack in his hand, the man pulled the draw-strings wide and tipped the contents onto his table. The Emerald bounced across the rough surface, glinting in the firelight.

"What's this then?" the man said in surprise. He shifted his bulk forward and picked up the gem to examine it more closely. "Could it be the famous Emerald?"

He jammed his bulging eye up close to it.

"Them birds an' that purple streak in the sky didn't just pass by for no good reason," he mused with growing wonder in his tone. "I knew they was lookin' fer somethin' big! Reckon that's what this is and it's mine now. Well, well, well, I'll just see what it can do for me."

He dropped the gem back in the bag and shoved it into his trouser pocket. "'Bout time I got some luck.

"When these two wakes up, I wants to question 'em," he said. "We can get rid of 'em later."

Scraping his chair back from the table, he lumbered to his feet, stumped to the door, and went out, banging it behind him. In his excitement over finding the Emerald he seemed to have forgotten all about his meal.

The woman breathed a loud sigh of relief. She limped past Kayden and dropped wearily into the chair the man had vacated, pulling a tattered apron up over her head to bury her face in her hands.

"Mercy me," she said through a sob. "What, in goodness' name, will happen now?"

Kayden felt it was as good a time as any to speak, so he opened his eyes, licked his parched lips, and said, "Hello."

The tiny woman perched at the table jumped several inches and squealed. Her apron flew up before she clapped her hands over her mouth with a worried glance toward the one window in the room.

She was as brown as the man, but her face was lined with the age of worry and care. Her hair was matted and grey, and fixed to the top of her head in a fat bun. She stared at Kayden, reaching to take one of the loose tendrils of her hair and twist it between her fingers.

Kayden could sense her fear and despite his desperate situation, compassion flooded his heart. This poor woman, from what he'd seen and heard in the last five minutes, her life must be a living hell.

He cleared his throat. "Hi, um, I wonder if you could give me a drink from my flask. I'm very thirsty."

She started again, her eyes flicking to the door, but she said nothing.

"He wants to see you as soon as you wakes up," she said finally, "but I will get ye a drink before I has to call him."

The little woman had made up her mind. Getting up from the chair, with a wince of pain, she began to rummage in Kayden's bag for the drink, then suddenly stopped.

"Mind ye do not tell him?" she requested.

"No. You can be sure I won't tell him a thing." Kayden rolled his head back and forth on the hard wooden floor for emphasis.

Rosalyn stirred with another groan.

"What's happening?" she said, her words slurred and weak.

"That's a good question," Kayden answered.

He regarded the little woman who bent to place the flask to his lips.

"Where are we?" he asked, before lifting his head to take a few gulps of precious water. "And why were we brought here?"

The liquid ran down his cheek and puddled on the floor as he dropped back with a little thud, but his throat was not so parched now.

The lady looked away, flustered. Straightening, she moved to Rosalyn's side and knelt down to give the girl a drink. Then she straightened and hobbled to the window to ensure the man wasn't near the door.

"Ye are in the residence of Andes Maloder, and I am his unfortunate wife Marta." She spread her hands in a gesture of defeat. "Andes used to work for King Larkender, tending his fields afore the trouble two years ago, ye understand. But he got caught stealin' an 'orse, among other things, and was banished under threat of punishment. Course I had to leave with him when he fled the castle, 'cause I is his unfortunate wife."

Turning, she looked back to the window to check outside for her husband, then went to the fireplace to poke it fitfully and toss in a few logs.

"An orse?" Kayden repeated, confused. "Rosalyn, what's an orse?" he whispered.

Marta came back to stand beside him. If possible, her face had grown a few more worry lines. "Be it true? That green rock me 'usband took from ye—was it indeed the great Emerald?"

Kayden could see no harm in telling this woman the truth since the man had already figured it out.

"Yes, but Andes can't be allowed to keep it. It's very, very important that I take it to the king. I mean, you're not on the side of Respiele, are you?" he asked, thinking perhaps he had said too much.

"Nay," Marta said with a decisive toss of her head. "I'm not on the side of that monster. Neither is Andes, for that matter. But none of that helps you I'm afraid. No, Andes thinks only of himself. He'll be thinkin' how he can use yer Gemstone for his *own* selfish wants."

She moved again to the window like a shadow, the ragged dress she wore swirling around her thin body.

"An' that is not good," she finished quietly, almost to herself.

Kayden didn't respond as he tried to figure out what to do next. He couldn't let Andes keep the Gemstone of Power, but he had no idea how to get it back.

"He be a dangerous man," Marta continued, shambling over to him again. "Andes robs any poor soul that tries to make it through Honistel Pass. Most times he kills 'em too. Flings 'em off the cliff, is what happens. Says it's cleaner that way. No mess." She heaved a deep, resigned sigh. "Likely that's what'll happen to you two in the end." She shrugged. "I'm right sorry about it. Especially as you're so young."

Great. This is just great, Kayden thought miserably. What was it his grandfather always said? 'Out of the frying pan and into the fire.' Yeah. That about summed it up.

"You could help us," Rosalyn said, her voice quivering.

"Or maybe we could even help you," Kayden added. "If you let us go?"

He looked at the scrawny limbs that protruded beneath Marta's dress and saw the reason for her limp. A length of soiled cloth was wound about her leg just above the ankle. It was completely covered in crusty brown blotches, apart from an area of bright red where fresh blood was seeping. It had been that way for several days, judging by the different colors and size of the stain.

"I see you have a wound?" he probed gently. "I could heal it for you. It will only get worse if you keep it wrapped in that rag. Infection will set in and then gangrene. It's horrible and painful and eventually it could take your life."

Marta's eyes grew large and then frightened. She plopped down on a chair. Pulling back her dress, she inspected the filthy rag about her leg.

Her face contorted with pain.

"'How you gonna fix it?" she questioned him suspiciously. "Ye got nothin' that can help me."

She struggled to pull her dress down to hide the wound, but failing, she stood up and hobbled over to the fire to warm her hands.

"Kayden *can* heal you," Rosalyn said. "He did it for me, but he needs the Emerald."

Marta swivelled about to look at her in disbelief. "The whole country knows what the Emerald can do, but who's him to have it obey his wishes?" She scoffed, tossing her head at Kayden. "I've just as much chance of healin' by askin' me own husband to do it."

"*His* name is Kayden," Rosalyn said, enunciating every word clearly and distinctly. "And he is the great grandson of Respiele himself, nephew of King Larkender and heir to the throne of Erinbourne."

Marta's eyes grew large and she looked impressed despite her obvious doubts. She lapsed into a brooding silence, then, pushing more errant hair from her face took a deep breath. She grudgingly nodded at Kayden with more respect.

"Aye, if what ye say is true, I beg yer pardon," she said. "But ye don't know what ye are askin' fer. Me own life is worth nothin' around here. How could I part Andes from the Emerald now without him killin' me too?"

"I think I can get the Emerald to heal you without either of us holding it," Kayden interjected, thinking of when he'd placed the Emerald under his grandmother's pillow and watched it work. "As long as you're as close to it as possible. But if it heals you, will you help us?"

Before she answered, Marta turned and limped painfully back toward the window.

The door crashed back on its hinges as Andes loomed in the opening.

"Where's me food, woman?" the man hollered, lunging into the room, and shoving her toward the fireplace. "What have ye been doin'? Get on with it!"

Marta spun across the floor, crying out in pain as she landed in a heap across from Kayden. Their eyes met for just a moment, but she gave him the tiniest of nods.

Chapter Six

Silently, Marta busied herself with preparing the dead rabbits for roasting. Her husband strode across the room and one by one lifted Kayden and Rosalyn up, still bound, and propped them in chairs he'd pulled away from the table. Kayden exchanged a long look with his friend, assuring himself she was okay. In answer, Rosalyn gave Kayden a smile which she stifled as Andes bellered at them from close range.

"I wants some answers." Andes dropped heavily into the last chair, scraped it up to the table, and pounded a fist on the worn wooden boards causing Marta to grab for the dish she was using lest it crash to the floor. "Who are ye and what's yer business up here?"

"We have no business," Rosalyn said sweetly. "My brother and I were simply travelling to visit an aunt living on the other side of the mountain. In Oglande."

The man's eyes narrowed. "Is that so? Strange time to be prancin' about the countryside, ain't it? Considerin' how war is about to be waged at the castle?"

"That is precisely why we took the shortcut across the mountain instead of going round the long way," Rosalyn returned smoothly. "It was scary down there on the roads with so many armies around. How fortunate we are to have met such kind and hospitable folks as you."

She smiled amiably, as though being drugged, hauled through a cave, trussed like a chicken ready for the oven, and tossed on the floor to rot was a courtesy extended only to the most favored of guests.

Andes' expression relaxed somewhat, until he recalled his purpose for the interrogation and rounded on Kayden.

"That might make a bit of sense, but what are ye doin' with the Emerald?" He reached over to prod Kayden's chest with a gnarled finger. "Eh?"

"I—I found it. In Norbern. On market day." He breathed a sigh of relief for coming up with something plausible. "Yeah, it was just lying in the street under an apple cart and I pic..."

Andes interrupted Kayden with another thrust of his hand, this time harder. "Yer lyin' to me boy," he snarled.

Taking Kayden's chin in callused fingers Andes lifted Kayden's face so close to his own that the man's hot, reeking breath billowed up Kayden's nostrils.

"But it don't matter, 'cause it's mine now."

Andes laughed. It was a dry, heartless sound that reverberated in the tiny cabin. Then, with his big, meaty hand, Andes stood up and struck Kayden, knocking him off the chair and sending him tumbling into a corner. Extending his arm again, he gathered the heavy folds of Rosalyn's cloak, picked her up off the chair, and tossed her there as well.

"I'll deal with ye after I eat," he said.

Kayden lay on the floor in a tangled heap beside

Rosalyn, but all he could see were her feet. There was no chance to talk. He could hear the sound of something being dragged and then a steady creaking noise. Must be the rocking chair, Kayden thought. He was facing the wall, but had to get turned around so he could see where Marta was in relation to the Emerald in Andes' pocket. He struggled and then gave up. If the gem was as powerful as he'd been told it was, it shouldn't matter.

Kayden waited until he heard Marta's limping steps toward the fireplace, knowing she'd be both bringing the meat to be cooked, and standing next to her husband. He heard the meat sizzle as it hit a hot pan and a metallic click as the pot was hooked over the fire. That was when he began to concentrate on reaching out to the Emerald and asking it to heal the woman.

Kayden was gratified to hear Andes leap from his chair yelling that his pants were on fire.

"What be happenin' here?" the man yelled.

Kayden heard him slapping himself, presumably thinking that a coal had burst from the fire and had landed on his leg. Then it sounded as if he had dragged the bag containing the Emerald out of his pocket.

"Why, it was the gem what got so hot just now," Andes muttered wonderingly. "That be a strange thing."

It should have done the trick, Kayden thought, pleased with his idea. He released the Emerald's healing power with a lifting of his heart, realizing as he did so that he was feeling very attached to the gem. Was it his imagination? Or could he feel the energy of the Emerald within his very core? Through Kayden, acting as the vessel, the Emerald was doing as its Creator had intended. It was happening slowly, but nonetheless it was healing the land.

Kayden knew, without seeing, that Marta's leg had been

restored. Still, it pleased him when he heard Andes growl at her again.

"What are ye doin' woman? Leave yer bandage alone. Quit wastin' time and cook my supper or fetch my knife an' I'll slice yer other leg to match."

"Nay, Andes," Marta said. "It's not likely to *ever* heal, I'm thinkin'. You taught me a real good lesson. Now, just a few more minutes and ye can eat."

Kayden wasn't sure how long he'd been lying on the floor waiting for Andes to pick him up, take him outside, and throw him and Rosalyn off a cliff—or so Marta had warned them would happen. He'd listened as Andes slopped rabbit stew down his gullet with much slobbering and slurping. Then he listened some more as the man glugged down what sounded like an entire pitcher of ale and belched a lot.

Kayden tried frantically to think of escape plans, but his mind rambled off to wonder why he hadn't even been offered a last meal before his execution and dreamed how easy life would have been if he hadn't agreed to help Durgot in the first place. Even school, with the likes of Dillon, paled in light of Andes hucking him off a mountain.

Stay on task, Kayden, he kept telling himself. *You're going to be killed! What are you going to do to stop it?*

But, to say his hands were tied was an understatement. What little feeling he had enjoyed in his arms and legs after being tied by Respiele's soldiers in Norbern, was nothing in comparison with being bound up by Andes the Mountain Man. He was having trouble imagining how they could escape, but hoped something would present itself. If it did, he and Rosalyn would be ready. Thankfully, he figured by now they should be able to count on Marta for help.

Finally, Andes pushed his chair back. "I'm goin' out to get the donkey. You help me load 'em, woman, and I'll head up the mountain. I got no use for kids," he spat, "and I don't want 'em hangin' around tryin' to get at my jewel."

His heavy boots clomped across the floor. "Best to just toss 'em to the birds," he said.

Chuckling at his own fiendish humour, he stepped outside and slammed the door.

Marta rushed across the room to Kayden. "It worked, young man! I thank ye from the bottom of me heart."

She rolled him over and started to work feverishly on his bonds.

"Now, hold tight and I'll loosen these off a bit." She picked at the knots. "We have to make the ropes look as though they still hold ye or he'll suspect me of treason…and we shall all be thrown over the cliff."

Releasing Kayden, she left him to rub life back into his limbs and scurried over to Rosalyn. Then, one at a time, Marta dragged both of them over to the door for Andes to load and handed each of them some dark-coloured bread. They tore at it hungrily.

"Ye need somethin' to eat fer strength if yer goin' to get away," she said, nodding at the food in their hands. "I cannot give ye yer sword since he'll be back in a minute and would surely know, but I can give ye back yer packs if ye can put 'em on quick like, under yer cloaks."

She handed them the bags with a furtive glance outside.

"And that little silver thing from yer pocket." She leaped to a chest under the window, extracted the boussole, and dropped it into his backpack.

"Thank you, Marta," Kayden said. He was deeply

grateful. The woman was doing so much to help them, to her own detriment. Who knew what horrors she would be subjected to once her husband found she had given back their things and helped them escape. "Could you go with us and escape?" he suggested. "What will Andes do when he finds out you helped us? I don't like to leave you here."

"Nay, I cannot go with ye. But myself is thinkin', now that I be healed up and all, that I might sneak away and go stay with me sister in Norbern." A look of hope crossed her face at this thought. "Yup, that be what I shall do. Thank ye young man."

With a wave of acknowledgment, Marta turned to Rosalyn, holding something out to her. "Andes' knife. I want ye to have it. It's in a sheath, and it's sharp."

Rosalyn took the knife and slid it under her cloak.

"Bless you," she said humbly.

"Hurry!" Marta whispered, peering out the grimy window once more. "Get yer hands back in the ropes!"

The door rattled and Andes flung it wide.

"Good," he grunted, his bulk filling the doorway. "I see ye made yerself useful fer a change, woman."

Together, Andes and Marta lugged Kayden outside and flopped him across the back of a bristly, brown donkey who stood waiting patiently at the door. The animal's ears flicked back with the monotony of it all. Clearly this was a familiar scenario for the animal.

Rosalyn was next. Andes flipped her on board, landing half on top of Kayden and facing the other direction.

Kayden struggled to catch his breath. It was hard to do, bent over double as he was and staring at the ground beneath the donkey's hooves.

With a muffled curse, Andes dragged the resisting animal across the scrubby grass and down a well-worn path.

Kayden raised his head to look at the house where they'd been. The tiny dwelling was nothing more than a one room shack, backed up to the mountain in a clearing of thin pine trees. As he watched, Marta darted to the house and vanished inside. He was sorry to see her disappear, but knew she was busy making good on her own escape. His eyes flicked up to where a column of smoke curled up into the clear blue sky and the almost comforting smell of wood smoke wafted along in their wake.

However, a chilly wind soon whipped it away into the deep recesses of the rock. Kayden shivered. He and Rosalyn were alone with a madman. He intended to fling them off the side of a mountain, and take the Emerald, the one artifact that could save the world of Erinbourne, for himself. The situation was desperate, but, by now Kayden had learned to stay optimistic. There was always hope.

He did wish he and Rosalyn had been able to talk though. How would the final scene play out? He had no doubt that Rosalyn would be able to handle the knife, but it would be nice to have a plan or be somewhat prepared when she pulled it from the sheath. But when? And what could one little knife do against such a huge and violent man?

His mind jolted back to the present. Lying on his stomach, across the back of a donkey as it picked its way along a mountainous trail, was a painful mode of travel. They made their way up the rocky trail and around a bend. Kayden's sense of hearing was heightened, despite, or perhaps because of all the blood that had rushed to his head. The cheerful chatter of chipmunks along the trail and the steady clopping of the donkey's hooves was rhythmic. He even noticed the mournful hooting of an owl and wondered why it was awake so early in the day.

Without warning, the animal they rode lost his footing on the smooth rock and came down on one knee. They lurched to the right. Rosalyn, who had slowly been slipping off that side anyway, slithered off the shaggy back to land hard on the stony path with a yelp of pain. With effort, Kayden lifted up his hanging head to check she was alright.

Andes stomped around to the side, hauled the donkey to its feet and cursing loudly, stomped to where Rosalyn lay. His huge body blocked what little Kayden could see, but as Andes bent to pick her up the forest came into view and a flash of white caught Kayden's eye.

This time, he saw what it was. A huge white owl flapped down from the sky, stretching out its sharp talons to grasp for a low hanging branch on one of the scraggily fir trees some distance from the path. The bird folded enormous wings behind its back, and sat motionless, observing them. It was far too large to be a regular owl though, and why had it been following Kayden for so long? Or could it be a coincidence that he had seen something white before? Kayden didn't think so. The round black eyes regarded him unblinking and then, as Rosalyn was deposited over the broad back of the donkey again, Kayden's face was forced down and he saw it no more. Andes yelled at the small beast of burden, and they swayed off down the trail. Yet Kayden could sense the owl's presence and knew, somehow, it was there behind him keeping watch.

Finally, after what had felt like hours of the painful flopping to and fro, they stopped. Andes plodded around to them, hefted Rosalyn up, and tossed her to the ground with a thud. Then, Kayden felt the vice-like hands seize him around the waist and lift him into the air like he was a doll before he was dropped beside her. Andes stepped back and looked at them.

"This is where ye meet yer maker," he said with a sneer and jerked a meaty thumb behind him.

Their eyes followed his motion to see they were sitting on a narrow ledge that jutted out from the mountain face where the trail ended. There was nowhere to go from here except back down the path or over the cliff, and with a sinking heart Kayden knew that was exactly their fate. The tops of shadowy mountains rose into the distance beyond the precipice. They were quite high up the mountain.

Andes crouched to pick up a large stone and shuffled to the brink of the void. While the big man's back was turned, Kayden began to loosen the rope around his wrists and feet. He could tell from her slight movements that Rosalyn was doing the same.

"Ye best watch that first step," Andes mocked. He paused just short of the cliff and swinging his brawny arms tossed the heavy rock off the edge for emphasis. "It's a right wicked one."

The stone was gone a long while before Kayden heard the faint smack of it hitting the rocks below. Andes twisted his mouth into what Kayden supposed was a smile, but it was thin and cruel.

As the giant of a man made his way back to them he stopped, reached into his trousers' pocket, and drew out the velvet bag. Andes yanked at the threads to force it open and tipped it into his hand. The shining Gemstone of Power dropped onto his palm. He gazed at it, his face softening with love and his eyes kindling with an Emerald flame.

Kayden had seen that expression before. It was a look of greed—born of a blackened heart, corrupted with the hope of untold wealth and power. Adlard had looked at it in just the same way and Kayden wondered if the Emerald would protest at its capture. Would it rebel in the hands of the enemy with the same intense heat as it had before?

But it was not to be, for Andes rolled it back into its cloth bag and tightened the strings about the top. Then he shoved it into his breast pocket so that only the rich golden strings were visible.

"That fool Ludwig Larkender, the so-called king, will soon know who is the most powerful," Andes muttered to himself. "And Respiele too. They will be sorry for how they treated Andes. Before I be finished, I will rule them all, and sit on the throne in Larkender Castle meself with a beautiful queen instead of useless old Marta…have all the horses and wealth I please. They will pay."

He patted the Gemstone in his pocket. Then with a start, he glanced up, seeming to recall the purpose for his trek up the mountain.

"Which one of ye is first to go?" he asked. Lacing his huge fingers together and cracking his knuckles in anticipation, he marched toward them.

Kayden tore his eyes away from the menacing man and stole a look at Rosalyn. She gave him the slightest of nods. She would wait until the right moment, and then would draw forth the knife Marta had given her and fight to the last of her strength.

So would Kayden.

He glanced back down the path for the great white bird and felt strangely bereft when he saw no sign of it. He and Rosalyn were truly alone.

Andes reached for Kayden first. His beefy hands closed around the cloak Kayden had been given and hoisted him into the air. The man moved quickly, as though he wished to be rid of them to get on with his plans for world domination. Kayden dangled from Andes' grasp, his toes dragging across the rock as they neared the edge of the cliff.

There was no reason to wait any longer. Kayden tore his hands and feet from the bonds and began to kick Andes legs and punch the man in the face and head, hollering to be let go. He struggled, squirming, and fighting, but Andes' hold was like steel. He lifted Kayden higher and shook him like a dog shaking a rat.

"Hey!" he yelled into Kayden's face. "'How did ye get loose?"

Rosalyn sprang to her feet and unsheathed the knife. She leaped across the stony ground and lifted the blade to plunge it into the broad back of her opponent, but her ankles had been tied for too long. She stumbled and sprawled onto the ground just as Andes flung Kayden, in a high arc, over the crumbling edge of the cliff.

"No!" Rosalyn shrieked in horror.

For a second, it seemed to Kayden as though he hung in mid-air, his mouth opening in a silent scream, his arms and legs pedaling furiously in an effort to fight his way back to the rocky shelf. Then, he plummeted toward the jagged boulders that rushed to meet him. The cloak billowed up to flap wildly around his ears and he clawed frantically at the air in an impulsive act of self-preservation, but there was nothing to grab hold of. Only empty space as he plunged to a swift and certain death.

Then his hopeless, terrified eyes caught sight of something large and white that soared down from the mountain, huge wings outstretched. He focussed on it. It was the owl— yet was not. As it hurtled through space, in the seconds before Kayden would have been dashed to bits on the rocks, it changed, transforming itself into a gigantic white horse that raced through the air with hooves flashing of silver. The horse dove beneath Kayden's writhing body to halt his doomed descent. Kayden collided with the horse's back, his neck snapping back and his back stiffening. Yet instinctively he clutched for the flowing mane that streamed across his face like a soothing balm.

Up the horse galloped, its silver-tipped wings beating powerfully, slicing through the atmosphere until, just a few meters from the ledge, Kayden saw Andes closing in on Rosalyn who stood on the brink of the collapsing cliff. She held the knife in front of her, slashing it back and forth in front of Andes' face as tears rolled down her cheeks. Kayden felt the horse gather itself to come alongside her, and sliding down the animal's right side, one hand wrapped securely in the silver mane, Kayden reached for Rosalyn.

Andes' eyes bulged as the horse appeared over the rock. He took a few strides forward to stop them, roaring with anger. The cliff edge broke away beneath his weight. Thrashing wildly in an effort to reach them, he pitched into the abyss with a howl as Kayden swung Rosalyn up behind him. Yet, as Andes fell, Rosalyn dove forward. With a flick of her knife she ensnared the long golden threads of the bag that held the Emerald and flipped it free. The blue velvet bag tumbled over their heads and winked out of sight into the chasm below.

Chapter Seven

Wheeling about, the horse laid his wings flat alongside his body and plunged in pursuit of the falling Gemstone. Rosalyn and Kayden were thrown back over the horse's rump and almost flew off. But Kayden gripped the horse's sleek sides with his knees and wound fistfuls of mane around his hands to keep them from tumbling into the chasm along with the Emerald. His ears popped with the change in air pressure. He didn't know how long he could hang on and was sure he was tearing the hair right out of the horse's neck as he used it to prevent him and Rosalyn from being swept off.

Although it hardly seemed possible, in mere seconds they were upon the bag and Kayden heard the click of large teeth as the horse plucked it from the air. Then he spread his wings wide, checking their descent, and glided along the cliff face. Far below, the black shape of Andes sprawled unmoving across the rock. Kayden averted his eyes. The horse lifted its wings and began to flap, pushing the air beneath him and carrying them up.

Clinging to one another and to the long silvery mane that streamed into the rushing gale beside them, Kayden and Rosalyn rose higher and higher into the heavens on the strong back of the flying white horse. Raggedly, they drew deep lungfuls of air. Rosalyn sagged against Kayden, her arms round his waist, her hands clenched into the folds of his tunic. Sobs tore at her body.

"I…Thought…You…Were dead," she finally managed to gasp into the whistling wind near his ear.

Kayden untangled one of his hands from where it gripped the mane and laid it across hers. They were both safe and, against all odds, the Emerald had been retrieved.

"You were amazing," he shouted back. He could feel her sobs lessen and finally her body relaxed as they passed the treacherous ledge and angled toward Mount Honistel. Each sweep of the feathery wings caught the air and smoothly folded it down to propel them across the sky. It was exhilarating and frightening all at once. Kayden's eyes closed against the draft, only to spring back open.

An unknown voice was addressing him in deep chiming tones that filled his ears like shattering glass. It was the beautiful white horse that had spoken.

"Prepare yourselves," the noble creature said through clenched teeth. "I shall land upon yonder peak."

Kayden narrowed his eyes to slits. The speed at which they were travelling made them water and the landscape hard to perceive, but he could see a plateau at the top of a smaller mountain, looming ahead. That must be where they were headed.

"Rosalyn, you heard that right? We're going to land over there." He pointed with a finger that wobbled in the wind with the speed of their flight. "Hang on."

Rosalyn shuffled closer to him and dug her hands

deeper into the material of his tunic just as they began to drop downward. The ground grew close at an alarming rate. The horse swooped over it and then his hooves touched down onto the sparse grass of the plateau and skidded to a halt. Breathing heavily, he folded his wings.

Kayden and Rosalyn slid awkwardly to the ground. The horse turned himself around to look at them and dropped the bag containing the Gemstone of Power.

"I could not carry that any longer," he said, eyeing the velvet package on the ground. "And, of course, we should be introduced, and decide on the correct action to take before proceeding."

"I am Thatus, son of Orielle, one of the Silpeth from the mountains of Mareele, at your service." Thatus stretched out one shining hoof and bowed his head low before resuming an erect stance, muscular neck arched, and noble head held high. He was huge, much bigger than an ordinary horse. Rosalyn stepped back and attempted a rather awkward curtsy as both she and Kayden bent their heads to acknowledge and honour the great horse. His large liquid eyes looked down on them and Rosalyn drew a deep breath.

"One of the Silpeth," she whispered. "No one in my family has ever seen one, only heard of them in legends told by our forefathers." She raised a small hand toward him, a smile playing about her mouth as she took a small step forward.

Kayden glanced at her and cleared his throat. She was awestruck, that much was clear. "We need to speak with him now Rosalyn."

Rosalyn fell silent, her eyes large as they darted toward Kayden.

He turned his attention back to the horse. "Thank you,

Thatus, you saved us from a terrible death back there. I am Kayden and this is Rosalyn," he said, extending an arm toward her. "We are very grateful that you came to our aide."

He stooped to pick up the Emerald and stuffed it into his breeches pocket.

"You are both most welcome and deserving of my aid." Thatus inclined his head. "And yes, I know who you are young Kayden, great-grandson of Respiele Larkender and heir to the throne of Erinbourne. News of you, and your gallant quest, has reached even our ears in the far Eastern reaches."

"You know about the…" Kayden paused, his hand resting over the gem. "Well, of course you do, or you wouldn't be here."

"The Emerald?" Thatus asked. "We Silpeth all know. It is the reason I was sent to watch over you as best I could."

"Were you following me as an owl?" Kayden asked, for confirmation of something he thought he already knew.

"It is true. I am able to shift my form to that of a snowy owl if the situation requires it," Thatus said. "However, we must speak of what is yet to come, for our time runs short."

During this exchange, Rosalyn looked back and forth between the two, listening to them speak. Finally, she lifted a hand to catch Kayden's eye.

"May I say something?" she asked, pressing her hands to her cheeks as she gazed upon the magnificent creature.

"Sorry, Rosalyn," Kayden said. "Of course."

"I just want to tell you how honoured I am to meet you Thatus. Thank you for carrying us." She then wrapped herself in her cloak against the bitter chill and subsided into silence.

Thatus lowered his head in acknowledgment. "Now, we must speak of what is yet to come."

The sun had begun to drop behind the craggy peaks to the west, and shadows were growing long upon the land.

"I shall do my best to carry you over the Honistel Mountain range and across the River Glee which lies in the foothills at its border," Thatus said. "Beyond that I can do no more. One passenger is achievable on a trek over summits such as these. Two, shall tax my abilities greatly. Also, on the other side of the river there is a dense forest leading up to the castle. There will not be any place safe for me to land near the fortress, and you could hardly expect to jump from my back in midair."

With a swish of his silvery tail, he twisted to look to the north. "From this point it is still several hours journey to the river, and I cannot fly in darkness. The light is waning. We must leave now, but I shall stop somewhere along the way for the night."

Kayden turned to Rosalyn.

"I am ready," she said, sounding more like herself.

Since Thatus was too tall for them to leap aboard, they found a sizeable boulder and graciously he positioned himself beside it. One at a time, they scrambled atop the stone to slide onto Thatus' broad back, being careful not to kick or poke him. Kayden wound his hands into the milk-white mane, spun with threads of silver. From behind, Rosalyn wrapped her arms around Kayden's waist. Then, Thatus turned his head toward the northern peaks of Mount Honistel, gathered his powerful hind legs beneath him, and thrust himself forward to thunder across the short plateau. As he galloped, the Silpeth unfurled the huge expanse of his wings. They caught the breeze that curled in around the rocks. Suddenly Kayden could no longer hear or feel Thatus' hooves thudding against the hilltop, for they had surged upward and become airborne.

It was glorious. Rosalyn released her grasp and flung her arms wide to the sky as they soared higher. Kayden, too, felt free. They were rid of Andes, somehow Rosalyn had managed to save the Emerald, and they were speeding through the air on a magnificent, winged horse. Kayden's heart soared. If he hadn't been afraid of attracting more attention than they already were, he would have whooped with exhilaration. As it was, he didn't make a sound, but he was happier than he'd been in a long while.

Dark patches of forest, craggy cliffs, deep blue lakes, and yawning black caverns skimmed past beneath them. While an occasional thin thread of foamy water splashed down from one of the many glaciers that capped the jutting peaks, but none of these summits were as tall as Mount Honistel itself. It reared up before them, showing the way.

Kayden made no attempt to talk, as it would have been impossible to carry on a conversation as they flew. Besides, the wind had changed. Before it had been a chilly breeze from the northeast, the direction they were going. It had now become a turbulent gale from the west, blustering about the mountaintops and bringing with it a bank of cloud, tinted with a faint hue of mauve that settled over Honistel and all the highlands. The massive mountain loomed to their right, pushing high into the darkening sky. It's very top vanishing into thick clouds that hung over the peak. They were black and ominous, each one reflecting the purple shade that rose in the west.

Respiele and his armies were coming. Kayden shook himself and frowned. He had no business being so happy in the face of that sight. The worst was yet to come.

The air became colder as the last glimmers of sun withered against the mountainsides. Kayden struggled to see ahead in the lengthening shadows. They didn't seem to be making much, if any, headway. Thatus' great wings beat steadily, carrying them ever onward, but they weren't as high as before and Kayden could feel the strong muscles of the Silpeth quivering under the strain. Thatus was weakening as the wind buffeted him, driving him back and thwarting his efforts. As well, the outlines of rocks that rose all around them were getting harder to distinguish. The journey to the river could never be completed in one long flight.

"I fear this ill wind blows in foul weather." Thatus said, his silvery voice easy to hear despite the turbulence.

Kayden leaned down along the animal's strong neck.

"If you see somewhere we could take shelter for the night, perhaps you should land," he shouted. But as he spoke, the first few drops of rain splattered onto his brow and rolled down his cheeks. Squinting, Kayden looked up. The clouds that had hovered over Honistel for the last hour, had swung down lower and now lay heavy over the earth, obscuring the tops of the mountains around them. In no time at all, the rain began in earnest. Each droplet cut a long, grey path through the sky to drop around them like the bars of a prison cell, unyielding and oppressive. It became almost impossible to see a few feet ahead, let alone spot a place to safely land on the mountains below.

Thatus angled his wings and they began to glide. His ears pricked forward and he dipped his head, turning it slowly from side to side as he searched for a break in the torrent of water that would allow him a window of sight to land. It was extremely dangerous to continue now that visibility was so limited. They slowed to a crawl, the rain beating them down lower and lower. Thatus slanted his wings to send them spiralling toward the earth. They were battered, pushed, and shoved as gusts of wind sent needles of icy water into their faces and down their necks, soaking them utterly and chilling them to the bone. It felt like an attack and they shivered with cold. Kayden clung to Thatus on their wild descent.

The storm grew even stronger, more intense. Thunder bowled across the heavens and lightning divided the sky in frenzied shards of light. Kayden lifted an arm to brush the water from his eyes, but it was hopeless. His clothes felt cemented in place from the driving rain that lashed at him. The droplets were huge, bombarding them from the sky and each one delivered angry slaps. It became difficult to think of anything else.

Thatus' hooves touched down, his legs buckled, then sprang forward, the momentum sending him galloping across the rocks. Kayden and Rosalyn were jarred from their hunkered positions on his back, but somehow they managed to hold on as Thatus slowed to a stop. His sides rose and fell with overexertion and his neck was bowed.

First Rosalyn, and then Kayden, slid off to stand beside the great Silpeth. Twice now he had carried them to safety.

They turned their backs to the lashing rain. Kayden drew his hood up over his head, for what purpose he didn't know, because it was as soggy as the rest of him. Though it seemed right to do something in an effort to stem the flood of water that continued to bite into him with a vengeance.

"This is no normal storm," Rosalyn yelled into the wind. "It is one of Malahd's wicked spells sent to stop us."

Kayden reached for her hand and gripped it tightly. He had no idea where they were standing, or if with one false move, they might step over the edge of a precipice and tumble to their death. They must stay still and close together. It would be too cruel after what they had escaped at the hands of Andes, to fall over a cliff now. A faint, silvery glow emanated from Thatus, but it was not enough to see where they were. Kayden knew, from the luminosity, that Thatus stood beside them. Only he couldn't be sure until he stretched out his other hand and touched the supple flank of the horse.

"I cannot see which way we should go, or if there be any shelter nearby." Thatus' voice again rang like a bell. Yet in truth, only the rain hammering onto the rocks and the rolling claps of thunder could have been heard by any ear other than that of a Garde.

They couldn't just stand there, torn apart by the elements, and neither could they see how to safely take another step. Kayden squinted into the gloom, but there was nothing but sheets of grey rain obscuring the world around them. The torrent pounded onto his skull until he felt like screaming.

Then, he remembered the boussole. If he could use its light, it might just get them out of this mess. Eagerly he flipped the sodden end of his cloak over one shoulder and struggled to drag the small pack from his back. Kneeling, he groped inside, sorting through the various items he'd carried since home. His fingers closed around a metal water bottle and several granola bars before his seeking fingertips connected with the smooth sides of the boussole.

Yes! He pulled it out and flipped it open.

Light sprang from the tiny open case. But something unexpected happened as well. It was as though Kayden had drawn a knife and sliced it into the air around him. The rain fell back instantly, as the boussole cut a path through the murk several meters wide in whichever direction Kayden chose to point it. Unbelievable! It was as though he carried an enormous umbrella equipped with a built-in headlight.

Kayden turned his attention wholly to their surroundings. Both open faces of the tiny magical compass whirled to life with a golden radiance that seemed to almost warm the air about them.

"What is happening?" Rosalyn asked. She looked up and extended both arms to wiggle her fingers. "Where did the rain go?"

It was as though the curtain of water had been drawn back by an unseen hand. Although it still fell all around them, the rain did not fall *on* them any longer, and she lowered her hands to wipe her dripping face.

"You are full of tricks," Rosalyn said. She grinned at him in the pale, shimmering light and Kayden felt an answering lift of his spirits. Thatus turned, shaking his head, and blowing air sharply through his nostrils to be rid of the moisture that ran in rivulets down his broad face.

"It's my boussole," Kayden said. He held it up for them to see. "Now we have to find shelter."

He looked back down at the small object lying across his palm. Two cogs within a square dial in the top portion were spinning like mad. He wondered if it was this that was hard at work to clear the air. He knew from Durgot's explanation that the upper half, showed direction, and worked in conjunction with the lower, rounded part of the boussole that gave light.

It stopped whirling. Kayden lifted it up like a flashlight.

"Follow me," Kayden said.

There were small rocks in the path, and he hesitated, but he had seen a shadowy wall of rock to the right of where they stood. Thatus clopped along behind Rosalyn, his hooves skittering over the wet rock and splashing into shallow pools.

Abruptly, Kayden stopped. The wall he had seen was an enormous boulder, part of what had been a long ago rock-slide. The boussole illuminated many other huge boulders that lay in a jumbled heap. Kayden shone the boussole up as far as the eye could see and then from side to side. The rockslide seemed to run in either direction. Making a decision, he led them to the right again. Stumbling along, with the rain slashing all around them, but not on them, they came at last to a recess in the rocks held open by a flat slab projecting out over top of it and protecting the area beneath from the elements.

With a sigh of relief, Rosalyn walked past Kayden. The area beneath the slab was not very big, but it would do as sanctuary for the night. She moved inside, leaned her back against the dry rock within, and slid down the wall to slump onto the heavy gravel under their feet. Kayden didn't move. The area beneath the sheltering stone was not big enough for Thatus. Yet even as he opened his mouth to speak to the Silpeth, to tell him he would stand outside with him, he could see that the horse was shifting shapes.

It happened in an instant, much the way it was with Talbot. One minute, Thatus had been standing strong and immoveable before them, his body huge, his hooves shimmering in the glow of the boussole, and in the next he began to shrivel. His body quivered and shrank, but his large black eyes never wavered. Within seconds, Kayden was looking at the huge snowy owl again. With a flutter of his wings and several graceful hops, Thatus entered the shelter and perched on a rock lying within.

"Are you coming?" Rosalyn asked, laughter crinkling her eyes in the dim, but steady light.

Kayden shook himself as surprise had rooted him to the spot. *Guess I should be getting used to this by now,* he thought, moving to join them with a grin. Thatus said not a word, but tucked his beak under one wing and promptly went to sleep.

Exhausted, Rosalyn was already making herself as comfortable as possible. She drew her pack out from under her saturated cloak and poked it a few times before laying her head down on the soaking wet canvas. Kayden did the same. He settled down with his back to the opening and his head level with hers. Slowly, he smiled at her with what he hoped was reassurance, and closed the boussole, extinguishing the light.

Thunder continued to crash around them, and rain pounded on the rocks outside their shelter without ceasing, but they were too tired to care. They were safe from Respiele's clutches for another night.

Tomorrow would bring its own peril.

Chapter Eight

Kayden opened one eye. A pale grey light was seeping through the gloom of early morning. He groaned and stretched before stopping with a painful yelp. What a whiner he'd been to complain about his old mattress back home. A bed of rocks was a heck of a lot worse.

With a grunt, he pushed himself up to sit and rubbed his aching shoulders. As he did so, he heard the clip clop of hooves and Thatus appeared around the outcropping of rocks. Only then did Kayden realize that the owl was gone, and Thatus, the majestic Silpeth, was back.

"You have awoken," Thatus said. "That is well, since we should be leaving this place as soon as possible."

Kayden snaked an arm back to rouse Rosalyn and met with the flat rocks of their shelter. He turned to see the space was empty.

"She's gone," he said with surprise, looking back to Thatus.

"Yes. She and I have been up for some time. The storm

has cleared and the path lies before us. Will you come now?" Thatus nodded in beckoning.

Kayden rose to his feet, grabbed his backpack, and walked stiffly out from under the shelter to follow Thatus around the corner of the rock. Fishing in his backpack, he found two granola bars for their breakfast. They hadn't eaten anything since the meager meal given to them by Marta.

Kayden strained his eyes, searching for Rosalyn across the short, flat expanse of narrow mountainside where they had landed the night before. One whole side ended in the wall of fallen rocks they had seen last night, and the other side was obscured by a thick wall of fog. Puddles of water lay everywhere and Kayden splashed a foot into one of them before thinking to watch where he was going.

"Where is she?" he asked, stopping to shake his foot. He was still cold and clammy from the soaking they'd gotten the night before. Having stepped into an ice-cold pool now didn't help matters any.

Thatus shifted his gaze toward the fog. An arm waved at Kayden from the thick of it and he stumbled towards Rosalyn.

"Beware the edge!" Thatus' said, but Kayden wasn't really listening. He drew closer to Rosalyn and the fog lightened a little, allowing him to see the cavern at her feet, yawning into the distance. Lurching to a halt he sucked in a sharp breath and stared across it.

Sunlight was just beginning to lighten the sky in some distant place where there were no mountains to block its passage through the sky, and the mist was receding, swirling below. They were level with distant summits all around them. All but Mount Honistel, of course. Its spire thrust into the dawn, catching the first rays of sun on its gleaming, snow-capped peaks. Kayden stepped back, further away from the edge.

"Are you crazy?" he hissed at Rosalyn. "Get away from there."

Smiling, she turned and strode toward him.

"Thatus is truly amazing," she said, not responding to Kayden's fear. She laughed out loud. "He landed here last night, on this tiny shelf of rock, in the storm, when he could see nothing! He must have *felt* his way down."

Clasping her hands together, she rolled her eyes heavenward and Kayden felt a fleeting jolt of resentment.

"You're right," he said simply. "Thatus *is* amazing."

Was he jealous of a horse? He handed Rosalyn the granola bar which she accepted doubtfully.

"What is this?" she asked, turning the bar over in her hand and fingering the tinfoil packaging with wonder.

"There's food inside," Kayden said. "Just tear off the wrapper."

Holding his bar up to show her, he ripped the foil and stuffed it into his pocket before sinking his teeth into the chewy treat. She looked at him strangely.

"There is much you must tell me when we have time."

She peeled the wrapping away and ate.

Together they walked to where the Silpeth stood, his nose raised to sniff the wind.

"Evil draws nigh," Thatus said. "Come, we must depart."

Quickening his pace, Kayden followed Thatus to a boulder at the foot of the rockslide with Rosalyn close behind. Taking turns, they mounted the Silpeth. Wasting no time, he wheeled around, preparing to leave. Rearing slightly, his powerful haunches tensing beneath him, Thatus sprang forward. This time, Kayden didn't feel the earth melt away beneath him, because the shelf they were on was not long enough for Thatus to gather the momentum needed to launch him and his cargo aloft. Instead, Thatus galloped to the edge of the precipice and with one mighty leap he lunged into the nothingness of the grey fog.

Rosalyn stifled a scream and, had his heart not already have been in his mouth, Kayden would have done the same. The mist was cold and wet. Swooping into it felt as though they'd taken a dive into a deep lake to which there was no bottom. Snorting, Thatus swam against the heaviness, his legs working as though still galloping. He spread his wings and worked them against the cloying air. Finally, they caught the morning breeze and beating his wings steadily and surely, Thatus lifted above the murky mass.

Soon, they were far beyond the dreary shadows of last night's storm and winging their way, once more, toward the great divide that marked Honistel Pass. Looking at the mountain range now, and seeing how far away it really was, Kayden couldn't imagine how it would have been doable on foot, as had been the original plan. They would have never reached Larkender Castle in time. Perhaps they wouldn't even reach it now, before Respiele and his evil forces attacked.

Thankfully, the sun lit the eastern sky and coupled with the wind, their clothes dried quickly. Although it was still cold. They drew their cloaks tighter as onward Thatus flew.

Whereas the day before it had seemed as though they were pushed back further than they edged forward, probably due to the enchanted storm, today was a different story. Mount Honistel steadily grew larger in their sight and soon Kayden could make out a winding trail leading up the western slope. From their height, the path looked as thin as the line of a pencil, drawn through a few spindly looking trees and lurching across a broken landscape of tumbled rocks and scrubby grass.

He looked off to the west. Nothing could be seen of the purple edged clouds that had hung over the mountains the night before. He was grateful, although he supposed it didn't mean much. Respiele always seemed to be close, 'breathing down your neck' as Gran used to say.

Apart from a few mountain goats, which Kayden pointed out to Rosalyn as they swept overhead, and a flock of crows that flapped by, taking no notice of them, there was not another living thing around. Below them, the trail continued although it climbed abruptly now. The pass was just ahead, the lowest point between Mount Honistel and its imposing neighbours. Although those mountains weren't as tall as Honistel, their peaks jutted into the sky like the craggy teeth of some monstrous being. It would be impossible to get over them. The only way was through the gap between.

Rosalyn slumped against him. Kayden could tell she was asleep. He took care not to jostle her, but eventually she stirred and looked around.

"This is it," she said. "The famed Honistel Pass."

Thatus plunged between the mountains, following a narrow channel formed in some distant lifetime. It felt constricted. Kayden found he was holding his breath and glancing to either side to make sure they would fit, as the passage was not much wider than the span of Thatus' wings. It was a tiny alley between the rugged edges of the two mountains, a dim and mysterious place that seemed rife with fear of the unknown. A coldness settled in Kayden's heart, and he longed to be out the other side and in the sunshine. Thank goodness Thatus was carrying them. They skimmed along the base of the pass, flying at an altitude not much higher than the rooftop of a house, since the passage narrowed the higher it went. Kayden could see the winding trail clearly as it made its way around huge boulders and across streams of black water that trickled out from beneath the mountain and seeped down its edges.

He hunkered down, Rosalyn doing the same behind him, and focused on the tiny pinprick of light at the end of the tunnel. The sound of their own passage seemed loud; the reverberation of Thatus' wings in the close air sounded like the slow beating of a drum. Then, they burst out the other side to freedom.

Kayden closed his eyes against the bright sunlight. Opening them partially, he saw the mountain range had ended unexpectedly, almost in a sheer rock wall on either side, and before them was a long expanse of green grass leading down a steep hill to where a deep, blue river flowed.

He patted Rosalyn's hand where it rested on his stomach and squeezed it tight. Thatus had brought them through the mountain. They could never have done it without him. Leaning forward, he placed a hand on the strong white neck of the Silpeth.

"Thank you," he said.

"I came to serve you in this quest, my future king," came the reply, but with his words came the overwhelming knowledge that Thatus was nearing the end of his strength. His voice was weaker than it had been the day before.

"Maybe the Emerald could revive you," Kayden said, wondering why he hadn't thought of it before. He reached out to the Emerald in his thoughts, asking it to restore the great horse.

"If I were injured or sick, then yes, I would request your assistance," Thatus replied. "But fatigue is not a malady that may be healed by the Emerald."

He dipped a little lower. They were only a few meters above the ground. Long lush grass swayed beneath them so close that, as Thatus faltered slightly, Kayden thought they were going to go down. But he knew it was Thatus' intention to see them safely to the other side of the fast-flowing River Glee. He left his hand on Thatus' neck, trying in a small way to encourage the winged horse.

After the tight, cold space between the rocks, the westerly breeze felt warm as it flowed over his face, but as he took a deep breath to refresh himself, a sharp acrid smell like burning chemicals wrinkled his nose. Then, he saw it— a wall of purple mist rolled over the surface of the river toward them, and riding near it were horsemen, five of them that Kayden could count, galloping along a well-used track in the shadow of the mountains.

The riders had also caught sight of Thatus, and with a distant yell, the thudding of their horses' hooves quickened. The heavy wall of mist sent tendrils of itself, like seeking fingers, looping through the air over the river and flooding its banks, carrying the riders along in its wake. They disappeared into the swirling vapours. But Kayden knew the riders were there and gaining on them.

It was as though the choking smoke from a prairie fire had taken on the twisted hues of purple as it wound high into the air, and cut a path through the long rippling grass toward them, weaving a sinister trail ever thicker and stronger. In mere moments, it was everywhere and still they had not even reached the water's edge. Thatus tensed and surged forward, redoubling his efforts to reach the river and cross to the other side before they met with the encroaching evil.

A few wingbeats sent Thatus hurtling forward. The grassland vanished as Kayden and Rosalyn winged out over the white sands of the shore. A fine spray of grit sifted over them, brought up with the surge of Thatus' wings as he laboured to keep up a ferocious pace.

Rosalyn clutched Kayden closer, and then they were over the water.

"It is going to take us," she said, fear causing her voice to squeak. She lifted a trembling hand and pointed.

The mass rolled along the water towards them, growing in size and power as it came. It bubbled in huge, swelling clouds as big as houses, and burst over itself to curl up once more, larger and taller again as it moved across the waves at an astonishing speed. Kayden and Rosalyn watched in horrified fascination as the colour saturated not only the air, but seemed to descend into the water and become one with the river. Purple caps began to form on the waves. They rose into angry peaks and rushed along the swirling waterway before sinking into the depths and leaping skyward again with increased size and fury. The coloured vapor curled up off the waves, thin fingers of it snaked out to search for them, almost sniffing the air as it sought the Emerald for the sorcerer Malahd and his master.

Thatus whinnied deep in his throat. His breathing grew laboured as he strove to rise into the air above the mists, but they were heavy and oppressing. His silver hooves dragged in the water, bringing up a spray that splashed over Kayden and Rosalyn as they clung to the great horse. He snorted and neighed as the psychedelic haze entered his nostrils, and stumbled, if such a thing was possible in mid-air. Thatus' head came up, and he tossed it, fighting against the mind-bending vapour and struggling to stay ahead of the thickening smog that twirled and twisted upon the water.

But still it came. The mist spun high into the air and then, drawing abreast of them, it flooded over and around them, seething about their bodies and trickling between them, separating them in their minds even though their bodies touched.

"Remember, it messes with your head," Kayden yelled to both of his companions. "Plants lies in your mind. Don't listen to it."

Like a prairie fire, the purple flames spread rapidly, appearing to devour the air in its haste to reach them. It sent plumes of violet coloured smoke curling down upon their heads.

Feelings of worthlessness swelled in Kayden's heart, and the utter futility of his life beat like a drum in his brain as the vapours caught up and eddied around them. His mind conjured up images of his persecutors back home, and the one in particular who had made his life miserable each and every day. *What was the use?* His head drooped in defeat.

Behind him, Rosalyn succumbed to the irresistible influence of the fumes. She slumped lifelessly against Kayden, slowly sliding to one side as her arms released their hold around his waist.

Kayden shook himself mentally and forced himself to focus on the Silpeth's faltering head in front of him. As though from a long way off and down an echoing tube, Thatus spoke.

"I…cannot…go…on much longer." His wings ceased to move, and he slowed, skimming lower and lower over the surface of the river. Then the purple mist fell over them in clotting waves, so thick they blotted out the world, leaving them in the dark silence of their own tormenting thoughts.

The steady thrumming of hooves beating on a hardened track entered Kayden's hazy brain, and he heard yelling although where and who it came from he didn't know. Then something whizzed past his leg. He felt it graze the material of his pants, stinging a little as it went, but then it was gone. Yet another of these things whistled by his ear. It felt like the harsh bristles of a brush parting his hair and sweeping past his ear with an angry hiss. His mind reeled. He forced himself to drag his brain from the mists and focus.

What was happening?

Without warning, Thatus screamed. His head dropped from under Kayden's hands, and his body crumpled. They hurtled down toward the unseen waves. Rosalyn tumbled up and over Kayden's head and disappeared into the mists without a sound. Kayden was frozen, his fingers lodged into Thatus' mane. His mind would not awaken. He sought to shake the fog from his mind even as he found himself sliding off after her, tumbling up through endless space. Behind him he heard a great splash and vaguely felt the spray of water. Somewhere inside, he knew that Thatus had disappeared into the wild river and was carried away in the gushing flood.

Chapter Nine

Kayden slammed to the ground. He rolled end over end, finally coming to rest on his back in the sand on the opposite side where the mauve-coloured river rose up to lap at his feet, in obedience to Respiele's demand. Kayden tucked his knees up to his chest. Shaking his head, as if in a dream, he became aware of Rosalyn, her legs tangled with one of his own. The smoky haze churned around them, growing in an intensity so compelling it took hold of each thought, exaggerated every painful memory, drew out every fear, and magnified them all. Kayden despaired. Thatus was gone and all was lost.

He drew a deep ragged breath and fought back. Slowly, he straightened his spine. He lifted his head to glare at the undulating purple flames, how he saw them now, that revolved along the water. They sought to blister his mind, and he summoned all of his strength to extinguish the consuming conflagration within. He would not let it happen again. The old Kayden might have given up and burned in this fire that was upon them, but new

Kayden had risen from those ashes. He closed himself to the vile thoughts that strove to creep into his brain and pushed back the fear that crept like a choking lump into his throat. The riders he had seen were there, he could feel them waiting for him, or even worse—maybe crossing the water to capture them both. Could Respiele's riders swim such a wide river? He lifted himself up to his elbows.

He and Rosalyn had to leave. They needed to get away from this place, from the men who had shot at them, and from this cursed mind-numbing trap. Laboriously, he reached for the boussole. It was closer at hand this time, in a tiny pocket at the front of his breeches. He pushed back against the tidal wave in his mind, forced his fingers into the pocket, found the cool edge of the silver compass, and drew it into the open.

With effort, he extended it at arm's length, far into the coloured mist so thick around them he couldn't see his own hand, placed a shaky fingernail under the rim, and flipped it open. The boussole sprang to life. It flickered into the overwhelming violet fog and the mist bowed to the power that shone into its midst. It parted and peeled back, sucking the swirling waters with it, and clearing a small area around him and Rosalyn. Kayden flopped back onto the sand, breathing heavily, and thanking Durgot and his magical silver gadget with every fibre of his being.

He rose to all fours and turned to Rosalyn. What he could see of her face, between long strands of her dark hair, was white as the winter snow. He smoothed the hair away and moved her arm from where it lay crumpled behind her head.

Clearing his throat he murmured, "Rosalyn?" Then more sharply, "Rosalyn wake up!" He bent over her, checking to make sure she was breathing. Her lashes fluttered and a frown of pain creased her brow.

"What happened," she groaned. She rolled sideways and coughed before sitting up and rubbing the sand from her face where she'd skidded onto the beach.

"Some of Respiele's men are on the other side of the water," Kayden said urgently. "They shot Thatus. They're on horseback which means they're faster. We have to get out of here before they kill us too."

"What!" She reared up, her face twisted with anguish. "Is Thatus alright? Where is he?"

She stared wildly into the swirling gloom that surrounded them.

"He's gone," Kayden said with an edge of pain in his voice. "Come on, we have to move."

Kayden lurched to his feet and reached out to help Rosalyn to stand. With the other hand he held the boussole high above his head and tried to orient himself, noting where the river licked the shore in order to know which way to go. Just out of reach, the vapours were thickening, waiting, and watching to overwhelm them again, and take control. As he looked away from the river to where he knew the forest must lie, he froze. Voices, angry and guttural floated across the water behind him.

"Where do they be?" said one in an irritated screech. "I cannot see through this cursed magic of Malahd."

"The Silpeth went down," answered a deeper voice. "My arrow pierced his side. Perhaps the riders were lost too. I could not tell."

"You had best hope the boy did not die beneath these waves, or there will be trouble!" said another. "We seek a young man such as that. The one who carries the Emerald.

Come! There is a bridge not far from here. We will scour the other shore and find him. Dead or alive."

Kayden placed a restraining hand on Rosalyn's arm, waiting until the sharp staccato of the horses' hoof beats faded into the distance before he felt it safe to begin scrambling up the riverbank. Tears ran unchecked down Rosalyn's face as she toiled up the hill beside him.

"I cannot believe Thatus is gone." She struggled to catch her breath between sobs. "He was so beautiful and kind. So strong."

"He was sent here to protect me—and the Emerald," Kayden said. "It's my fault he died."

He grabbed the stubby bushes that anchored their roots deep into the sand of the embankment, hauled himself the rest of the way, and bent over double, resting his hands on his knees. Rosalyn crouched down beside him, taking deep gulping breaths as she fought to control her emotions.

"This is not fair." She brushed a hand across her cheeks, spreading a streak of dirt from one side to the other.

"No, it isn't," Kayden said. Turning his head away, he swallowed hard. "But he died trying to save us, and Erinbourne. We can't let his death be in vain. We'll talk later. Who knows what else is coming after us in those mists. It may be worse. Let's head for the thickest part of those trees over there and get out of sight."

He gestured at the thick timber that lined the shore some distance away. They raced for the shelter of the trees. Kayden glanced over his shoulder to the east, hoping against hope he wouldn't see the ominous men on horseback looming out of the receding fog. All but a few lone tendrils of the smoky purple mist floated around them now, but Kayden kept the silver boussole raised. He wasn't taking any more chances.

As they advanced upon the great green wood before them, he chanced another look behind. The amethyst magic of the sorcerer hung over the river in great purple clouds to their rear, still clawing its way toward them in an effort to seize control once again. Yet, it was prevented from following them by the amazing silver gadget Kayden held in his palm.

Finally, gasping for breath, they slowed their pace and jogged into the shaded safety of the tall, dark evergreens.

"Any fool could trace our path from the water's edge to here," Rosalyn said between pants. "I don't know how we hope to outrun these servants of Respiele. They are on horseback!"

Kayden leaned on a tree to catch his breath. "Yeah, but they don't have dogs, so they can't sniff us out. This forest floor is covered with pine needles which might make our tracks harder to follow. We have a chance if we can run for a while. Plus, these trees are close together and they're much bigger than us. Horses would have trouble fitting through."

"I suppose we could always climb up them to hide," Rosalyn said.

Kayden threw her a quizzical look.

"The trees I mean, not the horses." She smiled wanly and began to weave her way through the densely growing trunks. "If the riders get too close, that is," she whispered back at him.

They concentrated on running as quickly as possible. Then, hearing nothing behind them for perhaps an hour, they began to relax a little. Although they didn't dare slow their pace.

"We should make sure we're going in the right direction," Kayden said. He slowed from a jog to a walk, motioning for Rosalyn to do the same, and consulted the boussole. It was not needed to part the waves of mist that sought to snare them any longer, but now required, as their guide.

Kayden breathed deeply, savouring his pine-scented surroundings, and looked up at glimmers of sunlight peeping through the tops of the heavy boughs above. It would have been impossible for them to determine which way to go if it were not for the tiny boussole coming to the rescue yet again. He concentrated his attention on the whirling needles and his heart lifted as they shuddered to a halt, pointing in a direction slightly northeast of where he and Rosalyn had been headed.

Nodding at Rosalyn to follow, Kayden adjusted their course. Thank goodness, Durgot had entered their final destination into the shiny gadget before handing it to Kayden.

"Thanks, Durgot," Kayden murmured.

Rosalyn stopped and looked at him. The silence was so complete in the forest, and their footsteps so muffled on the soft pine needles that covered the ground, that his softly spoken words had startled her. She moved closer to him as he consulted the hands of the boussole once more.

"This boussole you hold is very powerful," she said. "It holds back even the dark magic of the sorcerer."

She leaned in to look over his shoulder.

"I thought you would have seen plenty of them here?"

"I have heard of them, but they are quite rare." She reached out a tentative finger to touch it. "It is good that you have it to lead us since I have no idea where we are in relation to Larkender Castle."

She shrugged, then gestured that Kayden take the lead as they pushed off once more.

They ran again, after a furtive look behind them.

Kayden knew by now that Respiele's men would not give up easily and the closer they drew to the castle, the more desperate Respiele's need to secure the Emerald.

Several hours passed in which they alternated between a slow jog and a quick march depending on the terrain and density of the forest. The sun had passed high in the sky overhead and now began its slow descent into the west. Long shadows followed the trees across their path. They had just climbed to the top of a high hill when Rosalyn spoke.

"Shall we stop for something to eat and drink?" she asked. "I am thirsty."

Kayden nodded. Dropping to the ground, they each found a sturdy tree to lean against and took a moment to rest. Kayden unslung his backpack and dug into it for the flask of water that had been refilled by Marta at the nasty little cabin. He handed it to Rosalyn. While she took a few sips, he looked around, hoping to see the spires of a castle just over the treeline that surrounded them, but no such luck. He unwrapped a bundle of hard crackers they'd been given back at the Resistance camp. He was starving and could only imagine Rosalyn was too.

As they tore into the meager ration of food they allowed themselves, Kayden looked at the smoky blue mountain range rising low over the trees ahead. It reminded him of the Rockies back home, although perhaps not quite so high. There were so many mountains in Erinbourne. The boussole seemed to be steering a course straight toward them, so Kayden figured the castle must be nearby. Rosalyn followed his gaze to stare at the mountain range barely visible over the treetops.

"They are the Mountains of Tareele. Larkender's castle is built into the rock at the base of the tallest peak." She pointed. "There is only one entrance, which would be facing us if we could see it."

"Respiele's army is camped outside the gates," Kayden reminded her. "We can't get close to them, or they'll pick us up in a second. Have you been there? Is there a hill or some high spot near the castle where we could take a look at the situation and make a plan without getting caught?"

"Yes," she said, "there is such a place. It is a little to the west of that highest peak."

Kayden took the flask, had another sip, and replaced it in his pack as they fell into an uneasy silence, preoccupied with their own thoughts.

"We have crossed the first half of the River Glee, thanks to Thatus," Rosalyn added, hugging her knees, and bowing her head to folded hands. "And then we must cross the second arm of it again directly in front of King Lark-ender's castle. Much further east of where we are now, the River Glee splits. The northern half flows past the castle ahead of us, where it is fed by other streams that issue from the mountains. That is partly why the castle was built there. The river was a natural defence for the palace, almost like a moat. Enemies are forced over it to get to the king, and it is deep and fast so…it serves it's purpose well, I suppose."

"I see," Kayden said.

As Rosalyn spoke, his mind had been wandering back to the moment the great Silpeth had been struck down.

"We'd better keep going," he said finally. Shouldering his bag, he scrambled to his feet and waited while she did the same.

"Perhaps we could walk for a time?" Rosalyn asked beside him, raising her eyebrows.

"Yeah, sure." They started off down the slope.

"What is the name of this land you hail from," Rosalyn asked.

"It's called Canada. And I live in Alberta which is an area of that country. It's through the portal to the south." Kayden jerked a thumb in the opposite direction as though it were just across the road.

"Canada. Is it nice there? Nicer than here?"

She picked her way through the trees at the bottom of the slope.

"It's beautiful," Kayden answered without thinking. An image of his grandparents' farm popped into his mind as he spoke. He missed it terribly.

"We have a lot of things you don't have, like I told you before," he said. "But it's not necessarily better for that. I like it here too—or I would if we weren't being hunted down like animals."

He paused to lift a branch that trailed across their path and held it back for Rosalyn to pass. She smiled her thanks.

Rosalyn, ahead now, turned to stare at him before continuing on. "And how did you come to have a boussole?"

Kayden laughed, "Durgot gave it to me for this journey."

"Durgot? Ah yes, the Garde who keeps the southern portal secure."

Kayden peered through the gathering dim. The woodland ended abruptly, and a small, lush clearing unfolded before them. They paused before venturing out into plain sight, watching, and waiting. Tall, sighing grasses grew here, undulating back and forth like battered waves on the ocean before leading down a slight embankment to a pool that was fed by a gurgling stream. It sounded so, normal, Kayden thought, listening to water tumbling over rocks. On the other side of the stream, the same solid wall of trees continued relentlessly.

That was when he heard a horse snort.

Quick as a flash, Rosalyn scaled the nearest tree and disappeared into the branches. Kayden stood, rooted to the spot as fear gripped him. Then, lunging for a sturdy pine, he grasped at the rough bark and scrabbled for a foothold, leaping to snag the closest branch and haul himself up and out of sight. The branches scratched and pulled at him, but he was oblivious to the scrapes as he struggled to push himself through the dense needles. He just managed to pull his legs from view as a horseman appeared, the horse plodding as the man seated on its back leaned from the saddle, scrutinizing the ground. He was tracking them, Kayden realized, his heart pounding in his chest.

The rider came closer, weaving his way through the trees just as they had done, until he stood almost directly beneath them. He straightened and lifted his head to peer all about. Likely, he noticed their trail had ended and was wondering where they were. Kayden also guessed that the rider did not want to step into the open area without assuring himself of what lay ahead. He watched as the man, clearly a member of Respiele's army, since he was clad in the same sort of uniform as the others they had seen, leaned back, and fumbled with his belt. Then he pressed a small brass-coloured horn to his lips, took a deep breath, and gave a long blast that was cut short with a strangled yelp as Rosalyn dropped from above, hitting the man and knocking him from his mount.

Rosalyn was on the man like a wildcat and the skirmish was settled in seconds. She had the long black blade that Marta had given her and held its cold edge against his throat. He lay still, breathing heavily and glaring up at her with narrowed, angry eyes. Kayden slithered down the tree and landed lightly. Rosalyn sat on the man's stomach, her knee trapping one of the man's hands to the forest floor, the sharp point of her knife tilting his chin up. The tip drew a tiny trickle of blood that ran down his chin.

"Get his horse," she ordered, her eyes never leaving those of the subdued man.

Kayden leaped to do her bidding. Only it took some moments before he was able to talk the horse into letting him get close enough to grab the trailing reins, even though he was able to speak to it directly. He trotted the animal back to where Rosalyn held the captured man.

"Is there any rope on the saddle?" she asked tersely. "Mine is too hard to reach. Find something we can tie him with."

Looping the reins around a tree to hold the horse still since the animal was too agitated to reason with, Kayden discovered a coiled length of soft rope in a saddlebag. He flung himself to the ground beside Rosalyn and circled the cord about one of the man's thick wrists, and then the other, ignoring the curses the man spat at him. Kayden yanked the knots tight. Then, he pulled the rope down and repeated the process with the prisoner's ankles. Rising, Rosalyn helped Kayden to drag the fellow to a sturdy tree and pulled him up, so his back was against it before passing the rope around both he and the trunk. The man flung his body from side to side, struggling against the ropes and kicking.

"There," said Rosalyn in a satisfied voice. She rocked back on her haunches, gathered her hair, and flipped it over one shoulder. "Get on the horse. We have to leave. He was summoning others."

Kayden stood to his feet, hands on hips. "But we can't

just leave the guy strapped to a tree and ride off into the sunset," he said.

Rosalyn didn't have a chance to answer. The man's face curled into a twisted, mocking sneer and his eyes shifted to a spot somewhere behind both of them.

"Release him!" a voice said. "Now!"

Slowly, Kayden and Rosalyn turned to see who had spoken. Three men, most probably the ones who had brought down the mighty Thatus, were seated on horseback a few paces away. So stealthy was their approach, that neither he nor Rosalyn had heard them arrive. Two of the riders held heavy black bows, each with an evil looking arrow notched into the string and drawn back in readiness.

The leader lowered a heavy, double-edged sword and kicked his steed cruelly, moving him closer to hem Rosalyn and Kayden in. There was no escape.

Almost casually, Rosalyn rocked backward toward the bound man and lifted her blade to his throat. Kayden had to admire her. She acted boldly. Although what she hoped to accomplish with this move, when arrows were trained directly on them, was beyond his understanding.

"Lower your weapons, or before you strike me down, your comrade will die," she called.

"I care not. He is dispensable," the same man said. "But suddenly I find myself in need of a good rope. Now, drop the knife and untie him, or neither of you will live to see the morn."

Reluctantly, Rosalyn let the knife drop to the earth, but she did not move to do the man's bidding. She stood and faced the company with defiance.

"Okay, okay. Hang on," Kayden babbled, scared she'd get herself killed for this rebelliousness. "I'll do it."

He dropped to his knees and began to fumble with the ankle knots he had so recently made.

"Hang on," he called over his shoulder, "I've got to get the one from behind the tree first."

On all fours, he crawled around to the back of the fir, frantically trying to think of a way out of this latest fix. His eyes caught sight of something coming toward him through the lush meadow. The tall green fronds swayed, parting in a straight line as they were pushed aside to allow passage for whatever small creature it was, and while Kayden picked at the knots, he watched to see it appear.

A tiny black nose emerged from where the treeline ended and the grasses began, and then two beady eyes looked at him unblinkingly before one of them closed ever so slightly in a wink. It was a hedgehog.

Talbot!

The hedgehog sprang from his hiding place, curled himself into a ball, and flew toward the riders at a speed too swift for Kayden's eyes to follow. As Talbot rolled through space, he grew in both size and momentum. Long, deadly spines erupted from his body, and he became an instrument of dangerous proportions. The riders were dumbstruck, mesmerized with wonder at this strange being, and sat as though turned to stone. Their petrification was their undoing.

As Talbot came to rest in their midst, and unfurled his body to stand erect and menacing, Resistance fighters, with footsteps as light as the falling of autumn leaves, darted from tree to tree behind Respiele's riders of destruction. They stood with bows raised, poised to attack.

"You might actually want to look behind you," Rosalyn said to their captors. A pleased smirk spread across her face.

The leader was shocked at Talbot's arrival, but refused

to fall for a trick. However, one of his companions chanced a swift look behind and yelped with surprise. There was quite an assembly of the Resistance standing there, at least twenty of them. Each one held a bow with arrows aimed to kill. The bows were longer than their captors' and made of a light brown wood. There were men and women alike, all dressed in forest green from head to toe. Their faces were grim and hard.

"Throw down your weapons!" Talbot said.

The leader swivelled in his saddle to look back at the Resistance and then turned to Talbot who stood with his feet wide apart, spines bristling, and massive paws placed at his hips as he awaited their surrender. With a twisted smile of defeat, the leader tossed his sword to the ground where it clattered onto a rock. His three followers lowered their bows and allowed them to drop from their hands to the moss that grew beneath their horse's feet.

"You cannot stop the tide that is rising, whatever pitiful efforts you make," Respiele's disciple hissed. His jaw clenched. "Respiele *will* be king. It is only a matter of time now." His eyes darted to Kayden. "With or without the Emerald."

No one bothered to dignify his furious comment with a reply, but a few of the Resistance moved to gather the dropped weaponry while others stood watchful guard. Then, the riders were ordered from their horses, their hands were bound, and their mouths gagged before they were led some distance away. The man Rosalyn had captured was also taken.

Kayden looked at Talbot. He could have hugged the massive hedgehog if he didn't think it would have been a painful experience.

"I can't believe you found us!" he spluttered.

A broad grin lit up Talbot's dark face.

"Young man!" He strode to meet Kayden, laying his spines flat and sleek against his bulk. "I held doubt that we would ever meet again, but you have come far in the quest. And to have found a companion so well thought of by the Resistance, well…it is better than I dared hope! You have done well, lad."

Kayden's face reddened. He avoided looking at Rosalyn, because a sheepish smile had crept across his mouth.

"You know my friend Rosalyn? If it weren't for her, I would never have saved the gem," he said.

"Indeed, I do know Rosalyn." Talbot nodded. "She is not only the youngest of the Resistance fighters, but one of their finest. Wonderful to see you, my dear."

He gave her a slight bow, and she inclined her head with a smile. Then, looking about questioningly, Talbot addressed Kayden. "But where is your Runestaff?"

Kayden's face fell. "I left it in Norbern, during the battle that took place there. I'm so sorry," he said. His shoulders hunched. "I shouldn't have gone off alone, but I thought I could help the cause by setting fire to the catapult. Instead, I was caught by the enemy, lost the Runestaff, and the Emerald was taken."

"But it is safe now?" Talbot asked.

Kayden patted the front pocket of his trousers.

"Then all is well!" Talbot said. "We must make the best of it."

He turned as one of the Resistance members walked up to stand beside him.

"Excuse me, Talbot, sir," the man said. He nodded to Rosalyn and stared curiously at Kayden. "What would you have us do with the prisoners?"

"Three of our group will join me in walking them back

to Oglande where my present responsibility lies," Talbot said. "It is not far. The others will follow the river into the east and unite with our forces there."

"Very good," the man said, dipping his head in a signal of respect. He marched away through the trees to where they had assembled the prisoners.

"Now," Talbot said to Kayden and Rosalyn, "our paths must part once more."

He sighed and placed a clawed paw on Kayden's arm. "Travel as far to the north as you can. I would tell you to ride this horse, but it would not do you any good. The way is too steep and rocky from this point on. You still have custody of the boussole, correct?"

Kayden nodded.

"Good. Then it, and the knowledge that Rosalyn possesses, will guide you." He glanced up at the westering sun. "The light fades. You will not reach Larkender Castle tonight. Take time to rest, but do not trust the night to cover your tracks. Be ever watchful. There are others who may have heard the horn of the enemy."

"But...why do you have to go? And how did you find us?" Kayden asked.

Talbot sighed. "With help of others that were in Norbern that fateful day, I reached the Resistance camp shortly after you left. Naturally, I worried, when I heard you two had set out alone. But when I found that Thatus was following you, I rejoiced." He lowered his voice as though to explain something not even the trees should hear. "At times, we who serve the Guard may have privileged information.

"I was making my way to you by other routes, so, not too far behind." Talbot's voice took on a steely hardness. "I knew when Thatus fell. And...I knew how, and approximately where. The Resistance that were with me came to your aid in all haste."

His eyes took on a distant look, and he stared over their heads to a faraway place among the trees as though he wasn't with them any longer.

"Thatus was my friend," he said finally. "He will ever be missed."

"I'm sorry," Kayden and Rosalyn said simultaneously.

"It is the peril of war." Talbot exhaled and then fixed them with his glittering black eyes once more. "I must leave to ready other troops for war in the west, near Oglande. But I shall return on the morrow, at the castle, you may be sure of it. If our spies are correct, Respiele will arrive there early in the afternoon. With any luck, we shall be ready for him. Nonetheless, our efforts will be made useless unless you succeed in your quest. Everything depends on you. The Emerald must reach the king before the battle, or all will be lost."

Kayden rubbed a hand across his forehead. "To be honest, you make it sound pretty hopeless," he said. "How can we do this thing?"

"I do not have the sight to foresee such events." Talbot shrugged. "But I do know you are the only one who possesses the power to do it. I, and others, have faith in your ability, Kayden…and in that of your courageous, yet silent, companion."

He smiled down at Rosalyn.

Again, Kayden heard the words of his beloved grand-mother spoken through the mouth of another, 'I have faith in you Kayden'…'

He straightened his spine, pushed his shoulders back, and lifted his chin.

"I *will* do it," he said.

Talbot clapped him on the back, but then spoke directly to Rosalyn. "You must be given a sword."

She cleared her throat. "If possible," she said, "I would prefer a bow and quiver of arrows, sir."

"Of course." Talbot gave a long, low whistle and one of the Resistance ran up. "Give this girl your bow. She has great need of it. You may take one from the prisoners for now."

"Thank you," Rosalyn said, accepting the weapon.

The older woman ducked her head in acknowledgement before hurrying back through the trees.

Talbot pointed in the direction they should go.

"Farewell," he said. "We must not tarry any longer. All speed and good fortune to you both, young lad and lass."

Kayden lifted a hand to Talbot and with Rosalyn murmured a goodbye as they filed past the hedgehog and struck out across the grassy glade. Kayden darted a look over his shoulder as they reached the edge of the shallow stream, but Talbot was gone. Yet, hope leaped in Kayden's heart. Talbot had faith in him. He would do everything in his power to get the Emerald into the hands of the king or die in the attempt.

Chapter Ten

Kayden knelt on the pebbles by the rushing stream, reaching into a somewhat deeper channel to cup the water with his hands and bring it to his mouth.

Beside him, Rosalyn also gulped the cold, refreshing drink, wiping her wet chin with her sleeve before dipping her flask into the water. "Fill yours too. We will need it. Then we must press on quickly."

Moments later, Kayden backed away from the stream, took a run, and jumped to the other side. He waited for Rosalyn to do the same.

The meadow was not wide. Feeling exposed, they crossed it at a run. Warily they plunged into the dark green forest on the other side, disappearing.

As they trudged on, Kayden lost track of time in the shadowy world they found themselves in, but he knew they'd need to stop and rest for the night soon. The darkness and the silence around them had become crushing, yet he couldn't risk drawing attention by using the boussole for light. They hadn't seen or heard another living creature for a long time, not even an insect. The very trees themselves seemed on alert and watchful, waiting for the inevitable clash that was about to be unleashed in this world. With vigilance, they picked their way along. Too many things had gone wrong; too many forces had come against them to not be cautious now.

Kayden reached out and tapped Rosalyn's arm. He hated to break the ominous silence with his words, but he did it anyway.

"What about there?" he whispered. He pointed to a spot just ahead. Several trees grew closely together and their branches hung so low, forming a natural shelter.

"Yes," Rosalyn whispered back.

Dropping to their hands and knees, they crept, one after the other, under the heavy green boughs and into the yawning space created near the trunks.

"I like it," she muttered, appreciatively looking around. "We're completely hidden from view. Especially if we lie down to sleep."

"I'll take the first watch. You get some rest," Kayden said, sitting down with his back nestled into the tree trunks.

"Thank you." She yawned. Rosalyn wrapped herself in her cloak, laid between the old roots, and fell fast asleep.

Kayden woke in the grey dawn of morning. He was still slumped against the trunk where he'd tried to stay awake the night before. Cold and shivering from the damp, he pulled his cloak around him, but it was clammy too. He reached out to gently shake Rosalyn.

"Hey," he said, trying to master the chattering of his teeth. "Wake up. We have to get going."

He dragged the pack from where it lay beside him and

scrounged inside for whatever might be left that they could eat. One mushed granola bar, and some of the bread Marta had packed for them, were now crumbled. Well, at least they had something. His stomach growled. He'd been hungry for real food ever since being at the Resistance base.

Rosalyn pulled herself upright. They pooled their meager supplies and tucked in.

"You didn't wake me for a shift," she said, her mouth full. She reached for her flask.

"That's because I fell asleep myself."

"Oh…" She stuffed in the last bite, rubbed her hands on her breeches, and ran a hand through her hair in an attempt to remove some of the larger debris. "Well, we somehow made it through the night without a problem. It sure is cold though."

After washing his portion down with water, Kayden rose to his knees and crept out from their hiding space. Rosalyn followed. In turn, each one stood to their feet and stretched.

"Which way?" she asked, brushing off her cloak.

Kayden withdrew the boussole from his pocket and slid his fingers across it lovingly. What would he have done without it? In this dense forest, there were no landmarks to guide them. He flipped it open and watched as the silver compass sprang to life.

"This way," he said, striking out a bit further to the right than he would have thought was correct.

The trees grew so densely in this area that little sunlight was able to seep down through the boughs. Apart from the occasional hardy shrub, there was no other vegetation at all on the forest floor. It made their passage feel like a pole weaving contest. Kayden tried to walk faster, feeling their progress was too slow. Soon, however, the trees began to get sparse and the way became increasingly steep.

They climbed high enough that they began to see a craggy mountain range heaving into the sky ahead of them. As the trees released their foothold on the lower regions of the area, he and Rosalyn passed through fitful patches of shade offset by warmth from the sun. The heat beating on their backs, coupled with the increased climb, made for hot work, and they paused to drain the rest of their water from their flasks.

The terrain was rougher here too. It was getting more vertical by the minute. They slowed to pick their way over and around jagged rocks that had tumbled from above and lodged themselves in the ground many years past. The dense forest was giving way to ancient, wind-swept trees that had fought their way up the side of the lower mountain, growing evermore stunted and gnarled the further they grew up the mountainside. Until they quit trying to hang onto the rocks at all and gave up.

Despite having to watch his footing, Kayden's attention was drawn to tall, grey spires that pushed themselves higher into the sky with each step he took—Larkender castle. They were scaling a low mountainside directly to the south of it. Kayden sucked in a deep breath and stared at the awesome pinnacles that marked his destiny.

He squinted toward the sun and surmised it was probably around eleven am. He wondered what was happening at the foot of the castle right now. He grasped for a handhold on a jagged stone to haul himself up another step higher on the rocky ground. There was the odd, scraggly shrub for cover, but for the most part they climbed in the open now. They could easily be spotted. From the corner of his eye, he saw Rosalyn scan the sky every few seconds. He guessed she was watching for the flocks of starlings they had seen earlier in their journey—Respiele's spies.

This last leg of the expedition was necessary and the boussole had been unerring in leading them to it. From the vantage point of this small, weather-beaten mountain closest to the castle, they should be able to assess the grim situation that lay before them.

An angry wind picked up, skimming down the blue peaks and stinging Kayden's face and hands. With it came the muffled sound of voices from the valley that lay between them, and the castle that rose cold and dark against the mountain. Noises from the men in the enemy encampment, who waited patiently for the arrival of their leader outside the castle walls, floated up to Kayden and Rosalyn on the icy air. There was the steely clang of metal. Loud voices raised in anger as well as the constant stamp and movement of men and horses.

Rosalyn, who was far more skilled a climber, likely because Erinbourne was so mountainous, stopped, waiting for him to catch up before she spoke.

"As I told you, I have been here before," Rosalyn whispered, leaning toward Kayden, and shielding her mouth with a hand. "The spot I have in mind is just ahead of us now."

If the wind was carrying so much sound to them, she didn't want to take any chances it would carry their voices to their enemy, who would have stationed lookouts on these slopes.

Pulling themselves up the last few meters to the uppermost point of the mount, Kayden and Rosalyn dropped to the ground behind some spiny scrub, breathing heavily. Time to assess the situation. Kayden hadn't dared to look before, but now his eyes flickered to the amazing edifice built into the mountain face across from them. There, about a kilometer away, across the valley, and backed onto the Mountains of Calone, stood the mighty fortress of Erinbourne. Larkender Castle was massive. Three tall spires thrust into the atmosphere from near the mountain wall at the back. A series of shorter turrets projected at intervals along the curved outer face, allowing archers to protect the castle from these vantage points in the event of attack. Flags flapped in the chilly air from atop several pinnacles, but they were too far away for Kayden to see clearly.

At the base of the stone structure was a long, high wall running east and west against the rock, ending on the banks of what he now knew must be the second half of the River Glee. The fast-moving water wound its way along, only about thirty meters from the castle. Two huge, impenetrable iron doors were fitted into the wall to staunchly guard the inner sanctum. Leading down from these impressive doors was a slope wide enough to allow passage for a horse and carriage. It appeared to have been carved from the rock itself. From there, a cobblestone roadway, flanked on either side by patches of short green grass, coiled down to where a narrow bridge allowed access to the castle at the far eastern side of the valley.

Kayden paused, sucking in his breath. How was he ever going to cross this valley and get the Emerald to the king? On this side of the River Glee, hundreds of tents had been erected, and men scurried to and fro in the midst of them like a hive of angry ants. No doubt they were preparing for Respiele's arrival and readying for imminent attack.

Kayden shivered. What was he going to do? Breeze past an army of soldiers in the broad light of day, carrying in his pants pocket, the one thing Respiele wanted most in the world? Even with Rosalyn at his side, brandishing her knife and firing arrows, wasn't going to cut it. He had to think of a plan. Once again, the quest Durgot had given him seemed impossible. But by now, Kayden had learned one true thing —*nothing* was ever really impossible. There had to be a way.

He just had to figure it out.

Chapter Eleven

"The front gate is the only entrance I know of," Rosalyn said in hushed tones. They had been sitting in silence, staring at the outrageous task set before them. Then, voicing what Kayden himself had been thinking, she said, "But we cannot simply wander past several hundred men with the Emerald and cross the bridge. Even if it were possible, how would we get inside? Knock on the door and yell, 'We have the Emerald. Let us in!' It is madness."

She picked up a handful of gravel and heaving a sigh let it trickle through her fingers onto her pant leg. "Can we have journeyed all this way only to be stopped now?"

"Maybe we aren't...stopped," Kayden said in a low voice.

As Rosalyn spoke, he had been consulting the boussole and examining the rugged mountains to their left.

"The boussole is telling me to angle around the left side of Larkender Castle, along that mountain," he said, pointing. "What kind of a house would it be without a back door?" A grin lit up his face. "What do you think?"

He waved an arm toward the ragged peaks.

"I have never heard of such a secret entrance. But I suppose if there is one, and everyone knew, it would be a poor sort of secret. Perhaps there is a tunnel leading through the rock from the castle to a point beside or above it at the back?" In one swift move, she scrambled to her feet and shook the dirt off her cloak. "I say we trust the boussole and go. It has never been wrong before."

Kayden leapt up, and holding the boussole before him, they set off. Time was running out. Down into the scattered trees to the western side of the mountain they stepped as soundlessly as they could, and then up the other side. This landscape was easier to navigate, but now they knew Respiele's army was close. They made every effort to be quiet. Crossing areas of loose shale, they used the stunted scrub brush and pines to catch themselves from sliding as they made their way across to where the true climb would start.

"What about the river?" Rosalyn questioned, between breaths. "It runs through here somewhere. It has to."

She ducked under a branch and watched with concern as a small landslide rolled away from her foot.

Kayden had been keeping a close eye on the dials of his boussole. "We're up a lot higher than the river, here. Guess we'll know soon."

He grasped for a clump of dry grass to steady himself.

As it turned out, sounds of the rushing river met their ears long before they saw any sign of it. Emerging on a rocky outcropping high above the waterfall, they looked down through a narrow opening cut between the rocks. A fine spray was all that could be seen as the blasting power of the water sliced through the rock far below. It roared angrily.

"This is cool," Kayden said as he hopped across the gap and turned to wait for Rosalyn. "Nothing I do is ever this easy."

"Cool? Are you cold?"

"No. Cool just means—good. Things worked out well this time. They don't usually." He watched as she leapt across the fissure. "Not for me anyway."

Soon it became too difficult to speak. They concentrated on gaining hand and footholds, as they gradually worked their way up a safe distance from the assembled army in the valley below and began climbing across the rocks to an unknown point behind the fortress.

Painstakingly, they crawled and scrabbled their way around to where they could look across at the valley from the north. They rested for a few precious minutes behind a boulder. It had been an arduous trek taking a couple of hours, and their hands and knees were scratched and bleeding. Now had come the short climb down, to where Durgot's boussole was leading them. Kayden could only assume it was to the entrance.

"It's getting late in the afternoon," Kayden said, looking at the boussole. "And those troops haven't made a move down there. Guess Respiele hasn't arrived yet."

He leaned back and snapped it shut to focus on removing a splinter from one of his fingers.

Rosalyn sprawled on a rock beside him. "Where is this foolish back door anyway?"

"Not far now." Kayden consulted the boussole again and rose to his feet. "Come on."

Sighing, Rosalyn dutifully got up and slithered down a smooth boulder behind him, springing onto her toes at the bottom.

"There!" Kayden said, gazing back up to a point just

above where they had been standing. "Do you see that opening? It wasn't down here. It was just over our heads as we stood on that huge boulder."

He scrambled back up the gigantic, flattened rock. "At least I think it's a door." His voice echoed back. "Hurry! It's a cave."

The mouth of the cave was tall, wide enough for several men to walk through at once, and dark. Kayden paused before plunging into the gloom. Rosalyn took a deep breath and followed.

It wasn't so bad. Kayden had already released the pale beam of the boussole. While it didn't exactly flood the area with light, it was enough for them to see that it led off down an uneven passageway within the mountain.

"Walking into the unknown, usually down a dark corridor in a mountain, appears to be my destiny these days," Kayden remarked, as he tripped and reached out to the wall to steady himself.

Except his hand didn't meet with the hard unyielding wall. It met with something soft, and shaggy, and alive.

He screamed, swinging the light around to shine on the thing. It was gigantic—a huge furry mass—but it didn't move. Kayden lifted the boussole up higher and higher until finally it lit the glittering eyes of an enormous creature, standing like a silent sentinel beside them.

Rosalyn darted away from the creature and sprinted back to the doorway in competition with Kayden. But the cave's mouth was blocked by other creatures—*many* others. They shuffled robotically into a tight circle, effectively preventing either Kayden or Rosalyn from leaving or from even moving a muscle. Back to back, they faced a ring of the huge, hairy monsters. Craning his neck, Kayden looked into the face of the being closest to him. He judged the creatures to be seven or eight feet tall, every inch of them covered in long shaggy fur.

Silence hung in the dank cave. It was strange, but apart from moving to entrap them, the creatures had not made a sound, nor did they seem threatening.

"What are they?" Kayden said out of the corner of his mouth, tilting his head toward Rosalyn.

"They're called stiyaha. They live in these mountains, mostly hiding from people, I guess," Rosalyn hissed back to him. "I think they're pretty harmless unless you make them mad."

She tried to force a smile to her lips in the dim light, but failed miserably. One stiyaha positioned himself in front of Rosalyn and reaching out a huge hairy hand, he plucked her bow and the quiver of arrows from her back and snapped them into kindling. The pieces clattered to the stony floor amid Rosalyn's groans.

"Wonderful," she muttered. "What do they want with *us*?"

"Well, we're about to find out," Kayden said.

One grabbed him around the stomach, slung him effortlessly under its arm, and marched to the doorway of the cave where he stepped to one side and waited.

Another seized Rosalyn. She screeched and pummelled on the beast's stomach, but whether she liked it or not, she was lugged out the cave and down the rocks in front of the creature carrying Kayden. The rest of the beasts stayed back, watching from the hidden aperture.

Kayden reached out to them in the same way he had with the other creatures he had encountered in Erinbourne, first in his mind, and then, when that didn't work, he spoke out loud.

"Put us down." Nothing. "Can you tell me why you're

doing this, or where you're taking us?" No response. Their minds were closed to his probing. The stiyaha marched sturdily on.

With a start, Kayden realized they were the same beings that had attacked him and Talbot in the boat, shortly after they left Durgot's mountain domain. These creatures hadn't shown any of the animosity those others had displayed, but they did seem strangely bent on taking them somewhere—that much was for sure. They were fast too and appeared well-used to roving such rocky terrain. With a sure-footed gait, and long legs, they covered a lot of ground—rapidly.

Being carried wasn't too comfortable though. Kayden had been grasped around his middle, and both ends of him flopped awkwardly up and down as the stiyaha climbed back along the side of the mountain where Kayden and Rosalyn had just come, although they were taking a different route. Occasionally, Kayden's feet or arms would get smashed into the rocks as the animals trudged; Kayden could hear Rosalyn's muffled yelps of pain too. It was a nasty way to travel.

Soon, the pair of stiyaha made their way past the castle from a vantage point much closer to the fortress than he and Rosalyn had dared to negotiate on their way past, feeling they didn't want to attract the attention of either side. However, now Kayden could see the king's guards assembling within the castle's walls. These people were so intent on their work that they failed to notice two enormous woolly creatures trudge past, each one with a teenager dangling from his arm. King Larkender and his men were preparing for battle, which was good, but there seemed so few of them. For a while, Kayden entertained a wild hope that the stiyaha were taking Rosalyn and him into the castle themselves, and all his worries would be behind him.

It was not to be. The stiyaha soon left the castle behind, and with long strides, descended down along the rock toward the enemy. Kayden was getting worried.

"Where are you taking us?" Rosalyn asked the stiyaha holding onto her. "I hope it is not to see Respiele or his army? They are bad, bad men."

Rosalyn stressed her words, enunciating them slowly and distinctly as though speaking with a small child.

The creature did not respond.

"My back is hurting," Rosalyn tried again, in an obvious attempt to slow their progress. "Could you please put me down for a minute? I promise not to run away."

"Good luck if you did," came Kayden's dry retort.

Unbelievably, both creatures stopped, gently set their cargo down, and then stood stiffly at attention, staring out across the landscape with glassy, bulging eyes.

So, they must understand.

Rosalyn did a few stretches and touched her toes. Nodding at Kayden to play along, she spoke again.

"Respiele and the people that work for him are evil. Is that not true, Kayden?" She widened her eyes to encourage his response.

"Yes," Kayden followed up quickly. "They want to hurt us. Please do not take us to them."

Both stiyaha stooped over, picked Kayden and Rosalyn up once more, and continued making their way down to the enemy encampment. After a few more failed attempts to plead for their freedom, Rosalyn sighed.

"I believe they are bewitched," she said between gritted teeth as she flopped painfully at the creature's waist. "Have you tried talking with them...you know...using your ability rather than actual speech? I have. I could not reach them."

"I tried too," Kayden said between breaths as he lolled

under the stiyaha's huge, hairy arm. "*Oof.* I couldn't get anything from them. Not a feeling or a thought—nothing. *Ow!* It was like trying to talk to the side of a barn."

He craned his neck to see all that was taking place below. Their captors were drawing nearer to Respiele's camp at an alarming rate, reaching the River Glee in record time. Kayden wondered how the beasts planned to cross it, and hoped that perhaps they couldn't, and would set them down again. He planned to grab Rosalyn and try to escape this time. It was clear that the beasts intended to turn them over to Respiele, and if that happened, all would be lost.

Nonetheless, the stiyaha didn't hesitate. Turning abruptly, on a ledge that overhung the swiftly flowing waters below, the creature that carried Kayden lifted him into a more comfortable position, lunged up onto a higher ledge, and then leaped across the water at a point where it narrowed as it emerged from beneath the rock far below. Both stiyaha landed on Respiele's side of the River Glee, yet still high enough that they went unnoticed.

Great, Kayden thought. *Now what?*

He was near enough to see that Respiele's soldiers were arming themselves and forming lines of battle, ready to cross the bridge and wage war at a command. Between the river's edge and the soldiers, a legion of heavily armed men stood waiting—in their midst was Respiele. The stiyaha must have seen him too, for they halted and stood their captives on their feet while they watched the beginning of the war to end all wars. Kayden forgot all about his earlier resolve to escape as he stood mesmerized by his birds-eye view.

That has to be my great grandfather down there.

The figure was large and broad of shoulder. He was

clad in a shining breastplate and helm, like none other that Kayden had seen, emblazoned with the same elaborate letter 'R' carved and painted onto the shields of Respiele's men. Respiele's breastplate was polished to such a degree when it caught the occasional shaft of late sunlight that filtered between the mountain tops, became almost blinding to the eye. Respiele sat astride a gleaming bay horse that was similarly arrayed in silver armour. The beautiful animal pranced back and forth between the ranks, while Respiele barked out orders.

A chill ran down Kayden's spine. The man was menacing even at a distance.

Then, without warning, the great iron gates of the castle were flung aside with a resounding clang. Amid the blast of a horn, blown loudly from the battlements, Larkender's knights on horseback galloped in formation from the palace doors. Luminous light reflected from the polished shields the men held proudly before them and their horses wore metal plates upon their breasts and flanks. None were dressed extravagantly, like Respiele, but wore what looked like suits of leather, with chainmail fixed over the top half of their bodies and dull, metal helmets low on their heads. A few of them held a lance stiffly at their sides, but most held a shimmering sword.

As they cantered forth to clash with Respiele and the army he had taken years to amass, the vast doorway beheld one more defender of the Kingdom—King Larkender himself. He was dressed no differently than the knights who had gone before him, but Kayden knew at once that it was the king. A powerfully built horse carried King Larkender and strapped across his back was the Golden Sceptre of Power.

The king, and those who stood with him, cantered down the wide, cobbled entryway and reined their horses to the right, loping across the green expanse of grass that lay between the castle and the river. Then, shoulder to shoulder, they fell into line several horses deep, to face the onslaught that awaited them across the swirling waters.

Respiele's army marched forward, then knelt to draw their bowstrings back in readiness. They waited for one word from Respiele to fire, but Larkender also had archers. They moved into position from battlements above and from long slits cut into the stone walls of two towers that projected from the outer fortification at either end of the castle. Still more men poured from the castle gates on foot. They ran as a concentrated wall of defense behind the horsemen, swords held ready to strike.

King Larkender urged his horse forward, his hand upheld. Right to the water's edge he came and when he stopped, there was silence. Unbelievable as it seemed, the clashing and thrashing of the hundreds of men organising for combat, ceased.

"Brother!" King Larkender called in a booming voice that ricocheted around the valley. "Respiele! Come forth and speak. I ask, for the sake of us all, that you halt this war and make peace with me."

He waited, scanning the faces of the countless men that thronged the other shore.

Abruptly, the archers and assembled warriors fell back like waves from the prow of a ship. In their midst was Respiele, mounted likewise on his horse.

"There is nothing I would say to you, my dear liege," Respiele shouted. Sarcasm oozed from his raised voice as he rose in his stirrups and yanked cruelly on the reins of his horse. "You are not in a position to plead for an accord. Not now, after so many years and bitter enmity."

He laughed, a harsh sound that was like a chill wind sweeping through the valley. "There are so few here to fight for you. Perhaps that is why you beg. But let it be known that I have come to wage war upon you and all those foolish enough to stand alongside." Again he jerked on the bridle of his horse, sending the desperate animal rearing into the air. Respiele raised his sword above his head and screamed. "Strike him down!"

Respiele's forces struck. The air was filled with the sound of whistling arrows and the cries of battle.

Larkender retaliated. His warriors raised their shields and their archers fired into Respiele's ranks with deadly accuracy.

Despite additional defenses on Larkender's side of the river —riders with spears who stood barring the way at the mouth of the bridge, and the fact that the short length of drawbridge from the center of the bridge had been removed prior to the siege—Respiele's men got through. Kayden watched as heavily armoured soldiers ran to the bridge carrying what looked like boards strapped together with ropes. They threw it across the gap to allow passage across. Then Respiele's army poured over the top and flooded Larkender's knights on the other side. Others threw what looked like rafts into the river. These makeshift boats, carrying probably twenty men at a time, were shoved out into the current to land on the Larkender's side.

And with it all, Larkender's knights were slowly beaten back. As soon as they battled one group of combatants, another was there to take its place. Respiele had unlimited forces. It was not boding well for King Larkender.

Kayden's heart sank.

With a grunt, the first sound either of the stiyaha's had made, they snatched Rosalyn and Kayden into their arms and jumped from boulder to boulder down the steep edge of the mountain. Fortunately, with all the commotion, no one noticed their arrival. Kayden was sure Respiele would be pretty anxious to get over to him if the brutal commander had known that Kayden and the Emerald were near. The stiyaha reached the base of the mountain and strode toward the closest tent. In moments, Kayden and his precious cargo would be handed over to Respiele.

"Please don't leave us with them," Rosalyn said, making one last effort. "You don't know what you're doing…"

Her voice trailed away as the creatures stopped and gently placed them on the ground. Then, each one stationed themselves behind Kayden and Rosalyn and waited stiffly for a commander to give further instruction.

"What do *you* want?" A man dressed in the uniform of Respiele's agents of doom strode toward them. "Who are these kids? Clear off!"

Kayden felt hope leap, but then another man cantered up on a horse.

"Hendrik! This should be the kid with the Gem. Search him and report to Respiele."

The first man saluted his superior and rounded on the stiyaha. "You heard him! Get the Gemstone from this boy. I don't care if you have to rip him apart to do it."

Both enormous hairy beings moved in front of Kayden and one bent to grasp his arms. Kayden held up a hand.

"Wait," he said and his shoulders sagged. "I'll get it for you."

As he spoke, the gem started purring ever so slightly. Reaching into his pocket, Kayden withdrew the sparking green rock and ran a thumb across its smooth exterior. He'd come a long way with the Emerald and kept it safe thus far. Maybe there was just one last chance…

Kayden closed his eyes, concentrating on the Emerald and asking it to heal the minds of the stiyaha. Then, leaning forward, Kayden reached out and pressed the vibrating Emerald into the beast's huge, outstretched hand. Kayden folded the hairy fingers overtop it, and looked up into the creature's glazed eyes, willing the Emerald to work for him, one last time.

"Please help us," Kayden whispered.

The creature opened his shaggy hand and stared into the shimmering green depths of the Emerald. Flickering lights, like the rainbow effects of a diamond caught in a ray of sunshine, began to play across the beast's bushy face. His mouth opened and closed soundlessly. And then, a flurry of tiny translucent flakes fell from his eyes, dropping onto the thick fur of his chest. They looked like the shimmering scales of a fish, but only lingered a moment before disappearing like melting snow.

Blinking several times, the stiyaha lifted his eyes and truly looked at Kayden for the first time since their capture. A slow expression of recognition spread across his woolly face. Wordlessly, he dropped the Gemstone back into Kayden's palm. Then, the stiyaha gave him the briefest of smiles.

"What's taking so long?" the man demanded from behind him. "You fool! I told you to rip it from him!"

In a smooth move of pure, raw power, the stiyaha turned with a roar of rage to smite the sneering man. Respiele's soldier flew to the ground and lay still. Then, stepping over the crumpled body, the stiyaha bashed the superior officer from his snorting mount. The officer, who somehow landed in a crouch position, raised his sword, and swore, but the stiyaha swung his massive foot toward the man's chest, and lifted him into the air with a mighty, life-ending crunch.

"Go!" The stiyaha wheeled back to face Kayden and motioned for him to run. Then, roughly, the creature grabbed his companion by the arm, and dragging him across to the trees, they disappeared within.

Chapter Twelve

"Come on!" Kayden yelled at the stunned Rosalyn.

He had started to run but stopped, realizing she wasn't moving. She was paralyzed, rooted to the spot in shock. He wheeled around, grabbed her hand, and yanked her to life. Together they sprinted to take cover behind a tent. Another contingent of men, preparing to cross the river and join the multitudes that were already part of the battle, saw them, and yelling, rushed toward Kayden and Rosalyn. Respiele's army surrounded them on every side except the river and Kayden made a snap decision born by necessity.

"We'll have to swim across," he said, panting as they ran. "You *can* swim, right?"

"Yes," she choked, "but not *that* far. And there's a strong current here!"

"No choice." Kayden checked over his shoulder. They were closely pursued and would be caught momentarily if they didn't do something, and fast.

Stopping at the water's edge, they tossed off their cloaks and packs, before plunging in. The icy flood took Kayden's breath away and pulled him under the swirling water. The rushing flood carried them both away from shore toward the bridge. Kayden came up spluttering. Frantically treading water, he searched the surface of the swirling waves for Rosalyn, and his heart unclenched a little as she popped up downstream and gulped a breath of air. He swam to her, using the current to reach her side faster than she could float away. Then, they both started the difficult task of swimming back against the flow. As long as they were in the water, they were safe from the soldiers. No one would dare kill Kayden where the Emerald could be swept away forever.

But could he and Rosalyn make it to the other side? They now had a fight to swim across, and they were weakened from lack of food and rest. Chances were they'd wear out fast. Besides, even if they made it to the other shore, they couldn't just leap out in the thick of the fighting and expect to remain unseen. Kayden's mind boggled at all they had to surmount before they could get through the fighting and deliver the Emerald to the king.

But first things first, Rosalyn was right. It was a wide river, and strong. He raised one arm after the other and fought against the undercurrent with his legs, but he could soon tell Rosalyn was tiring as quickly as he was. He saw her face just as a large wave rolled over her head and submerged her. She looked desperate. He wasn't able to speak nor even summon the energy to check on her after that. Every ounce of strength he possessed was expended in the effort to keep himself afloat. But it was no use. Their bodies had been through too much already. They were tired, their arms and legs becoming limp as noodles as the cold penetrated their bones, causing muscles to tighten and painfully contract. And worse, glancing up as his head rolled to take a short breath, Kayden saw they were barely halfway there. It was hopeless.

Something bumped into Kayden's leg, but he was past caring. Then it banged into him again and a second something thumped into his side. Kayden's confused brain tried to piece together what was happening. Were they being attacked underwater somehow? Was it fish? Now another was under him. It moved toward the surface, buoying him up. He found himself resting against the unseen force, too weak to fight back as it took over and began to propel him steadily for the other shore. He took a deep, shuddering breath and searched the tossing waves for Rosalyn. She met his eyes with the same look of wonderment as he supposed was evident on his face. Then the being, for he could feel its legs pedalling beneath his chest, pushed Kayden's face right out of the water. A large black nose come up for air beneath his chin, and he saw two small flat ears on either side of a sleek brown head.

Beavers!

Kayden would have laughed for joy if he hadn't been so worn out. Thanks to Camden and Edna, they had been saved! Such noble animals, these beavers! Kayden made a mental note to personally thank each one he saw when he got back to his grandfather's farm.

With surprise, he learned there were more beavers than just the pair he knew. Many of them swam beside him and Rosalyn, surrounding them, paddling sturdily beside them, ensuring they were safely borne across the river and deposited on the other shore. Kayden lifted a feeble arm from the water to point at the spot he felt they would be most hidden, and the bevy of beavers took them straight to it.

"Thank you," Kayden and Rosalyn each managed to

whisper, just before the animals sank soundlessly beneath the rippling waves and were gone.

He and Rosalyn crawled onto the bank and flung themselves onto their backs, panting in the tall reeds that lined the shore. Yet Kayden knew, without a doubt, the group of men that had seen them with the stiyaha would be racing across the bridge in hopes of alerting Respiele to Kayden's presence. There was no time to lie around. With his teeth chattering from cold and fright, Kayden lifted his head and looked at Rosalyn. She stared back at him with sorrowful eyes and a slight shake of her head.

"I have nothing to fight them with," she whispered. "The knife was all that was left, and it was in my bag."

She flopped a weary hand into the mud over her head.

"It's alright," Kayden replied. "We'll to think of a way. We're so close."

Coming up onto their elbows, they dragged themselves forward, inching along until there were no more reeds in which to hide. A few willows afforded them a little cover, but not much, and they stayed hidden on the ground a second more to evaluate their chances of making it to the king.

War waged all around them. Swords clashed, men and women strained and grunted, arrows pinged through the air, and horses neighed in terror. People from both sides lay across the battlefield, bloody and broken. The King and his closest knights fought bravely, though it was easy to see they were sadly outnumbered, and their prospects looked bleak. Fresh combatants swarmed across the bridge from Respiele's camp every minute to take the place of others who had been vanquished. Out of the corner of his eye, Kayden caught sight of Respiele himself as the man rode forth to challenge King Ludwig Larkender.

Respiele charged across the bridge, aiming a deadly

spear at his enemy, while a sword lay ready at his side. Ludwig had not seen Respiele's advance. He focussed his attention on two well-trained assailants who were intent on cutting him from his horse and seizing the magical sceptre for their master.

Swiftly Respiele galloped, despite the fighting on every side, and only at the very last did King Ludwig hear the thunder of hooves behind him. Deftly, the king managed to rein his horse to one side just before Respiele's sharp blade pierced him through. The metal only grazed the king's side. Yet, Respiele's horse smashed into Ludwig's own steed with enough force to unseat him from the saddle. The king tumbled to earth.

Respiele leapt from his horse to face his brother with a howl of triumph. He lunged at the king, but Ludwig was already on his feet. Their mighty blades clanged as they dealt one another blow after blow.

The sound rang hollow in Kayden's ears as he watched in fascinated horror. Finally, Rosalyn nudged him, motioning they should get moving. He nodded, and they began to crawl around the west side of the broad grassy expanse in front of the castle, keeping a wary eye on all that was happening only a few arm lengths away.

Pride for the king surged in Kayden's heart. The king was tall and strong, wielding his polished sword with a skilled hand, and upon his back rested the Golden Sceptre of Power. The deep blue Sapphire and the blood red Ruby flashed in the westering sun as King Ludwig fought the man who had mindlessly resolved to destroy him. With the Gemstones of Power held close, courage and strength rested on his side, and none, not even Respiele with all the anger and hatred his twisted mind had fashioned, could stand against the king.

Nonetheless, Respiele was cunning. His armour shielded him against every blow. The metal looked thinly made, allowing him to move easily, yet no arrow or blade that came against it was able to penetrate. Respiele parried, matching the king blow for blow, thrusting, and falling back only to lunge forward to strike again as he watched for an opportunity to deal a final clout, surrounded on every side by the violence of war.

Deflecting a charge from Respiele, King Larkender drove at his opponent with speed and agility, taking him off guard. He knocked the sword from Respiele's hand. The weapon dropped with a thud to the grass and Respiele bent over backward as Larkender held the shining tip of his blade to his brother's neck where the chest plate and helmet had parted to expose his throat. Around them, soldiers continued to fight, oblivious to the epic battle waging beside them—but Kayden saw it all and leapt to his feet. This was the moment he needed.

He dashed forward with Rosalyn at his side, running and leaping over the fallen. They dodged swordsmen intent on their destruction and swerved around those who had neither weapon nor hope. Desperation was etched upon the faces of both sides, and wounds too great to heal pumped blood from bodies broken.

Stooping as she ran, Rosalyn plucked a sword from the hand of one who had no use for it any longer. She held it, ready to defend Kayden's wild rush to fulfill his quest. Yet, none stood in their way. Kayden, his gaze fixed on the goal, imagined how he would end all of their struggles as he thrust the Emerald into the king's victorious hand. Then would come the joyous moment when all this torment and turmoil would end...

But it was not to be. Both Kayden and Rosalyn ground

to a halt and watched in dismay as a twisting purple cloud coiled its way down from above and hovered over the King. Kayden's eyes flicked up, tracing its origins back to the bridge.

A cowled shape stood upon the overpass. Respiele's soldiers, who had been making their way across, in order to fight, had fallen back to allow room for this dreadful figure to pass. No one dared come close, not even those who fought for this person's cause. Almost casually, the figure held a short, straight, silver cane in his hand, and the vapor curled up from a glistening purple stone set in an elaborate filigree at the tip.

"The Amethyst," Kayden breathed, dropping to his knees. "Oh no."

"Malahd," Rosalyn murmured, her weapon still upheld as she took in the scene.

As the smoky, purple shadow flooded across the battle-field, each hand it caressed was stayed, and each head bowed to the torment it caused. Kayden knew that inner turmoil well, but the coloured ribbon did not come for him this time. A stillness fell upon the fighting men. The effect spread outward like the widening ripples of a pool disturbed with a stone, and in that moment, every face turned toward the king, Respiele, and the feared sorcerer, Malahd.

Panic clawed at Kayden's heart.

King Ludwig's hand that held the blade to Respiele's throat never wavered, but he raised his head to seek out the source of this foul magic that spun its web about him.

"Your conjuring has no effect on me Malahd," he said, his voice strong. "My mind cannot be broken."

"I have no interest in your mind," Malahd hissed. The vapour poured ever more thickly from the tip of his cane, gathering itself to coil and wind itself around the King.

"Remove your filthy stain of deceit or I will kill your master here and now!" King Larkender said, forcing the subdued Respiele lower into the grass. But his voice lacked conviction. It was his brother after all.

Could the king truly kill Respiele?

"Do what you will," Malahd jeered. "Are you quite sure *who* is master here?"

Malahd moved then, almost as though he floated above the ground. The Amethyst spun wildly at the tip of his staff, shooting a lavender flame up to trace a livid arc across to King Larkender where it descended with a sizzling sound upon his head. And then the power of the amethyst came together, transforming itself into a cord, fluid and supple, that darted in and around the king as he stood poised over his childhood rival. With a snap of his staff, Malahd tightened the lavender rope like a whip, and brought King Ludwig crashing to the ground.

The king strained against the sinuous strands that held him captive. Snake-like, they continued to wind and tighten, threatening to squeeze the very life from his body. He screamed for his men to save the sceptre, but the amethyst kept them immobilized.

Malahd focussed his malice and the mauve mist concentrated, feeding all of the sorcerer's power into the rope that bound the king. Released from the Amethyst's grip, the knights of King Ludwig and the armies of Respiele went back to their fighting, but it was easy to see that the defenders of Erinbourne had lost hope. There were few guardians of the Golden Sceptre of Power left standing, and those who still stood lost courage at the sight of their beloved leader, overthrown and helpless on the ground.

Respiele rose to his feet and straightened, rubbing his neck, a smile curling his cruel lips. He bent to pick up his sword and flipped it into the air like a circus showman before catching it again. In triumph, he swivelled his head to gloat at those around him—and spotted Kayden.

With a cry of rage, Respiele rushed at him.

Kayden jumped to his feet, his only thought to somehow evade Respiele and reach the king. He crouched, unsure of which way to move. Rosalyn prepared to guard Kayden, brandishing her sword. Then, several things happened all at once. A revolving black monster emerged from the river's edge and hurtled past Kayden. Every inch of the beast was covered in long, lethal spikes, and as it careened past, it hurled a long grey stick into the air.

"Catch!" the hedgehog bellowed, before launching himself at Respiele, bowling him over into the grass.

"Talbot!" Kayden yelled with relief and joy. Jumping, he extended his arm to catch the Runestaff.

The strident tones of a horn split the air. Kayden, gripping the staff, swung his head, following the sound. He gaped in astonishment at what was happening on the river and across the other side.

Boats and rafts of all shapes and sizes were floating down the river and nosing into the banks on either side. On board, countless numbers of men and women were poised and ready, armed with whatever crude weapon they had mustered. Some were farming folk carrying pitchforks and axes, while others shifted long, lethal scythes from hand to hand. Many of them had only shovels or simple garden implements, but each was pledged to the king's service and to Erinbourne. All were deadly when in such numbers as these. They surged ashore with a shout.

Then, from the east came riders galloping, their long brown cloaks flying in the wind behind them and Sonalia was leading them. There were more than a hundred of them. Rosalyn clutched Kayden's arm with one hand and with the other she thrust her sword skyward in solidarity.

The Resistance had arrived!

They drove into Respiele's forces with a vengeance, forcing the enemy away from the bridge. Respiele's soldiers fell back in shock, struggling to regroup and meet these new combatants.

Then another development caught Kayden's eye. He pointed to a flowing brown river that poured down the nearby mountainside and spilled into the valley. It was a storm that flattened everything in its path; an angry, seething stream of life that took no prisoners, but exacted a deadly payment for wrongs done. Kayden looked up in awe as hundreds upon hundreds of stiyaha thundered down the hillside. They were everywhere. They swarmed Respiele's men, dominating them, devastating their ranks, and laying waste their schemes.

Kayden's heart leapt at this fresh hope, yet he knew it was premature. Malahd still held Ludwig and would claim the sceptre soon if it hadn't happened already.

How could I have forgotten the king?

Kayden wheeled around, just as Rosalyn looked back over her shoulder, a shout of joy ending on a strangled cry deep in her throat. Behind them, Respiele had arisen, and Talbot was nowhere in sight. From within his shielded helmet, Respiele screamed with anger and bounded toward Kayden. Two of Respiele's soldiers ran before their master, determined to achieve victory on his behalf.

Grasping her sword with both hands, Rosalyn stepped in front of Kayden, planted her feet, and crouched like a coiled spring, ready for battle. The first of the soldiers struck, but she dealt him a blow that brought him to his knees. Rosalyn poised to face the next attacker.

Kayden watched Respiele, ready for the maniacal man. Thrusting the staff over his head, his eyes narrowed. Wrapping his fist around the wood of his Runestaff, he focused on a symbol he remembered seeing near its base, one he could picture clearly in his mind—the image of a falcon.

The stick contorted, its shape shifting, expanding, and bursting forth up and out of his grasp. It sprouted feathers and a great hooked beak opened wide with a piercing cry as it dove away and flung itself to Kayden's defense. The bird fixed its enormous yellow eyes on Respiele who recoiled in his tracks and stood motionless in the face of this new development. The winged terror was huge—the size of a horse. It settled on the ground between Kayden and Respiele, its gigantic wings outstretched, its head bent low and menacing. And, in his mind, Kayden knew what the falcon was asking him to do.

A surge of adrenalin galvanized Kayden into action. He sprang toward the enormous bird and flung himself onto its back, grasping the rough feathers around its neck. It hunkered even lower to the ground, gathering its strength and then, with an ear-splitting cry, launched itself into the air just as Respiele charged at them with sword outstretched. Respiele slashed into air as they veered over top. He had missed his chance. The massive beating wings drove the man backward onto the turf.

The falcon was off, winging its way into the air. Kayden tilted his head forward against the powerful neck of this mighty bird of prey, leaning into the gusts of wind as the force of gravity fought against their steep vertical climb, trying to drag him back to ground. From above, they circled once around the scene as Kayden took in the grisly sight.

Far beneath him, the war waged on. There were far more of Respiele's troops than Kayden had realized. He could see the lone figure of Talbot defending the bridge against any that would oppose him. Rosalyn battled Respiele's warriors alongside members of the Resistance that had arrived in the boats. Now with the influence of the Amethyst had focussed elsewhere, the flames of battle had reignited, and in the midst of it all, the fight for the sceptre burned red hot.

Malahd hovered only a few meters from the King. The thick purple ropes that had sprung from his cane had not only bound and restrained the King, but now had suspended him several feet off the ground. The monarch's body hung limp in the Amethyst's snare and his feet dangled uselessly in midair.

Respiele rejoined them. He gazed up to where Kayden and the falcon were but a speck in the sky, paying them no heed. Once Respiele had the Scepter in his grasp, it would only be a matter of time before he called every Gem of Power to his side, including the Emerald, wherever it happened to be. If Respiele took possession of the scepter— he would most certainly rule Erinbourne.

Wind howled past Kayden's ears as he hung to the bird's strong neck. He squeezed his eyes shut and buried his face in its feathers.

Would he continue to allow bullies and fear to rule his life? None of this journey had been easy. He'd been afraid plenty of times, but he'd learned a lot about himself. For one thing, he was more resourceful than he'd thought—and not nearly so cowardly.

It was time to take a stand.

Kayden's thoughts reached out to the bird just as they had done to the staff, linking with it, and translating his requests without need of utterance—almost before they were barely thoughts at all. The Runestaff understood what he needed it to do. Kayden pushed his hand into the pocket of his sodden pants, and one last time, withdrew the Emerald. He clutched it between his fingers, knowing it was now or never. As one, Kayden and the falcon ceased their ascent into the clear blue sky, spun around hard, and plummeted to earth like a vengeful spear of justice.

Chapter Thirteen

Just as a bird of prey tucks in his wings and drops upon his victim, so was it that the pair dove from the sky toward Respiele, the wizard Malahd, and the king for whom Kayden had travelled so far. The wizard's enchanted hold on King Larkender must be broken. In the mere seconds it took for them to careen to earth, the falcon had extended its gnarled talons, aiming straight for Malahd and his silver cane. The talons connected with their target and knocked the sorcerer sideways as he moved to secure the sceptre. Malahd sprawled across the grass, losing the tight grasp he held on his cane, and on the Amethyst. It was only for a moment, but it was enough.

King Larkender fell heavily to the ground; the purple bonds had been broken. He lay gasping for air like a man who had been held under water, but he was free. Kayden's fearsome fowl landed lightly and bounded across the grass. Its enormous wings hammered on Malahd, talons ripped at the wizard's cloak, and the yellow beak dove at his exposed face and hands. It plucked him up and flung him away in an effort to keep him apart from his cane a second more.

Kayden leapt from the bird's back. There was still Respiele to contend with. The man crouched beside the weakened king, his hand upon the sceptre, his lips twisting cruelly.

"You have lost," Respiele said with a sneer, tugging at the leather holster that housed the Golden Sceptre of Power.

Kayden took a tentative step forward and hesitated, every sense heightened. Respiele, his attention focussed on the sceptre, reached with both hands to unfasten the heavy leather straps across Ludwig's back. Now was the time for Kayden to act. His peripheral vision caught the gleam of the king's discarded sword lying nearby. Swiftly, Kayden snatched it up and heaved it, end over end, at Respiele.

Even as the sword left his hands, Kayden ran after it, leaping over several prostrate forms lying on the turf. The Emerald had come alive. It was humming with electricity and sudden warmth, leading Kayden on. The Gemstone of Power pulled his arm taut, straight as an arrow in front of him as though it were being drawn by a magnetic force to the sceptre, and he followed in its wake.

Ahead of Kayden, the sword hit its mark. With a howl of pain, Respiele fell back from a gaping wound in his thigh. His face twisted with fury, and he swore with frustration, forcing himself upright again in a frantic attempt to release the straps and secure the sceptre. But now Kayden was there too, and the Emerald had taken over.

The green gem was not just vibrating, but spun in his hand with such intensity and heat that Kayden could not hold it any longer. He opened his fingers to free it and the stone rose into the air, hovering for a fleeting instant, before it whirled through the air in a blinding flash of green light and snapped into its rightful place on the head of the Golden Sceptre of Power.

Respiele was flung to his back with the force of this reunion. He gripped his bleeding leg.

At this time two things began to happen. Malahd recovered his cane and was facing down the falcon who refused to budge. With massive wings outstretched, the falcon blocked his path, impervious to the magic of the Amethyst that curled about it.

And, nearby, King Larkender was slowly rising to his feet. In fact, it wasn't so much that he was rising of his own accord, he was being lifted to stand. With a life entirely of its own, the sceptre blazed on his back, humming like the droning of a thousand angry bees. The jewels revolved crazily in their positions on the ornate, crown-like setting, sending multi-coloured sparks shooting into the atmosphere like a miniature display of fireworks. As though suspended by unseen hands, the king drifted upward. His head lolled from his shoulders, his arms drooped forward, and his body slumped. He appeared lifeless, but the sparklers lit upon him, enveloping his body in colour and light, sizzling before penetrating the king's frame. His body shuddered, as though ridding itself of a great sickness, and he lifted his head.

Almost mesmerized by the colourful antics next to him, Respiele tried to drag himself away from their influence, but he couldn't get quite far enough. The tiny embers showered down around him, engulfing him in the same way they were submerging Ludwig. Each tiny glittering light glowed briefly on Respiele's metal suit before soaking inward. He gave a great moaning sigh before collapsing back onto the grass.

Within seconds, Larkender had gained enough strength to stand on his own. He stooped and retrieved his sword.

Still carrying the sceptre in its harness on his back, King Ludwig drew himself up to full height and faced Malahd, who had recovered his cane. The twinkling power of the gems subsided.

"The balance of power appears to have shifted," King Ludwig said quietly, his eyes narrowing as he looked from Respiele to Malahd. He transferred his gaze back to rest on the wizard. "Your assistant appears to be suffering some ill-effects of the gems. I suggest you award the Amethyst to its true owner."

King Ludwig extended his left hand, palm up, while assuming a battle stance with his feet spaced wide apart, sword held ready in the other. He watched Malahd carefully in the lengthening shadows.

Kayden's falcon stepped aside with an inclination of his noble head. Malahd was not beaten yet. Tilting his cane toward Respiele, he spoke several commanding words into the wind.

"Aneelah mareesh tuniel!" Malahd lifted the Amethyst, calling upon its ability to bend the minds of those around him.

But nothing happened.

"Arise and fight, you fool!" he shrieked at Respiele. Both gnarled hands clutched his cane as the wind grew ever stronger, screeching through the valley to pick up his long purple robes and swirl them around his feet. The strange mauve mist that preceded his every move rose around him, thick and suffocating.

He levitated several inches into the air and flew at the motionless Respiele. The falcon rose squealing behind him, but the powerful bird could not penetrate the choking mist that clothed the evil magician like a heavy mantle. Respiele was jerked to his feet by an invisible power. He hung there as his sword rocketed upward and was thrust into his hand. Gripping it limply, he swayed, held aloft on unseen threads, compelled to do the bidding of the crazed magician.

"Now we shall see," Malahd said with a menacing sneer.

He flung Respiele at the king, with a wide sweeping stroke of his cane. Respiele became rigid as he soared through the mist, electrified by the authority of the Amethyst and its wielder, as he landed on his feet near Larkender. He was forced to engage in this clash that had been years in the making.

They faced one another in this preordained battle to the death. The king stepped forward, slashing at Respiele, the enemy he'd never wanted to have.

Respiele parried. He moved with the studied motions of an automaton, stiff, unbending and seemingly unaffected by his injury. Back and forth they went, neither winning nor losing. And all the while the mist settled around them like a shroud, lingering patiently for the time when it could condemn the loser to death.

Nearby, Malahd watched this scene of his own making with pleasure, moving closer to the fray, urging his creation to fight harder, adding vigour to his limbs with the incantation of words muttered beneath his breath. Malahd dangled his puppet Respiele by a gossamer thread of hazy mauve smoke, orchestrating the man's movements and assuring himself of victory.

Then Malahd paused, seeming to tire of this amusement. Edging nearer to Respiele, he thrust the cane, capped with the blazing purple Amethyst, closer to Respiele's body. Respiele tautened with renewed strength.

"Strike him down and be done with it," Malahd hissed.

Without a word, Respiele obeyed. Twisting his torso

back on himself, groaning in agony with the battle between the sorcerer's magic and his own will, he lifted his great shining blade and brought it down with all the force he could muster—on the arm that held the Amethyst.

Respiele collapsed, lifeless. A blood-curdling shriek of pain and rage issued from the gaping mouth of Malahd, shattering the valley as the Amethyst dropped from his grasp and the wizard's staff fell with a thud onto the cold, damp earth beside his severed hand. In the seconds of shock that followed, Larkender spanned the distance to the sorcerer's cane and snatched it up. Gyrating with amazing speed, the Amethyst wrenched free of its golden bonds on the magician's stick, and whirling through the air like some tiny, purple meteor, it joined the other precious gems on the sceptre of the true king.

King Ludwig Larkender flung himself down beside Respiele as Talbot and Rosalyn came rushing to their aid. Kayden, who felt as though he'd been turned to stone, came to life and ran toward Malahd in a vain effort to stop the sorcerer before he got away. The falcon spread his wings and launched himself up, extending his huge, clawed feet, but both were too late.

"I will return," shrieked Malahd, his hate-filled eyes swivelling to include King Larkender and Kayden both. "And when I do, you both will die." Uttering a scream that ricocheted around the mountain peaks, the sorcerer vanished in an ebony cloud of smoke. No longer in possession of a Gemstone of Power, he had called upon whatever black magic he possessed in his arsenal to make his escape.

In the ensuing silence, the falcon, with a haunting cry of victory, transmuted back into the humble Runestaff and slammed into Kayden's outstretched palm.

Chapter Fourteen

The body of Respiele was lain to rest among his kin in the castle graveyard on the morning of the second day after the end of the war. Sadness hung heavy on the shoulders of his brother, King Ludwig. No one except Kayden and the king mourned for Respiele, but they had been with the man in his final moments. They both knew at the last his heart had been set free of the poison that had warped it.

Throngs of people had filled the churchyard to bid farewell to all of the brave warriors who had been lost in the battle. They honoured the fearless folk who had come when they were needed the most, and fought valiantly for friends, family, freedom, and their king. It had been a sombre, motley group that attended the mass funeral. The beavers and stiyaha were there in full force. No one had ever seen so many of the latter together at one time, but desperate times had necessitated that all creatures under the sun in Erinbourne join together as one. Thatus was remembered too as Talbot had stepped forward to speak in tribute of his friend.

Kayden, however, felt terrible. He'd slumped beside

Talbot and Rosalyn on the hillside as King Ludwig had spoken comforting words to his people. Kayden worried that perhaps he had somehow killed Respiele—his own great grandfather.

Afterward, Kayden voiced his fears to Talbot as they walked slowly back to the castle.

"Nay, young man, you are not to blame," Talbot said. "It was Respiele's own thirst for power and control that led him down a path of self-destruction. He was foolish enough to seek the aid and council of a sorcerer. But soon became a slave to Malahd and the sorcerer's own twisted plot to overthrow King Ludwig and assume command of Erinbourne. While everyone thought Respiele was in control, in fact it had been quite the other way around."

Talbot slipped a comforting arm around Kayden's shoulders. "You see, I believe the true Respiele died long ago. Since then, he existed only because Malahd willed it to be so, using the power of the Amethyst. Respiele was a servant, a pawn, a mere shell of the man he had once been, but he was useful to the sorcerer and thus, was allowed to live. When Respiele came into contact with the authority of the gems, he was freed from Malahd. Drawing upon what strength of his own will he had left; he did his best to end the sorcerer's reign of destruction. But...there was not enough of who Respiele once was to keep him alive."

"It is all so sad," Rosalyn said, trudging behind them on fallen autumn leaves that carpeted the trail. "So unnecessary."

"War always is," Talbot replied.

Talbot, having remained in his gigantic form since his arrival at the castle, thumped Kayden on the shoulder as he entered the great hall that same evening for a celebration and feast. The happy blow sent Kayden sprawling into Merlot, the chieftain of the stiyaha's, and the one on whom Kayden had used the Emerald. Merlot stood silently near the huge wooden doors as still as a statue. After apologizing to the shaggy stiyaha, who inclined his head graciously, Kayden grinned at Talbot and shuffled inside to find an empty space near the east wall from which to view the proceedings.

Deep contentment flooded over him. The hall was huge and filled with those who had given of themselves for Erinbourne and their king. Some, such as the stiyaha and a few remaining beavers, stood outside, too uncomfortable with so much human interaction to step within the castle walls.

Kayden's heart was full. Although he was sad for what his great-grandfather had done and how the man's life had ultimately ended, Kayden now understood it wasn't his fault. Hastily, he brushed away a telltale tear that escaped down his cheek and sighed. His eyes roamed over the familiar faces gathered in the hall, and who had played some part, large or small, in his quest. He considered each of them in turn.

Even though the other stiyaha remained outside, away from the gathering, Kayden couldn't help but think of them. What remarkable creatures they were! In a brief conversation he had enjoyed with Merlot, Kayden learned that Malahd had paid the chief stiyaha a visit, many months ago, in his mountain cave. Merlot couldn't remember much after that, until Kayden had placed the Emerald in Merlot's hand. The shackles that had bound him to Malahd's dark magic had fallen away. After that,

Merlot had only to touch each one of his kind to free them as well. It didn't take the stiyaha long after that to unite and make their way back to the castle to stand with the king.

Then there were the beavers. Kayden smiled. That very morning, he had spoken with Edna and Camden, and properly introduced them to Rosalyn. Camden told Kayden how he and his wife had left their lodge the morning after Talbot and Kayden had departed on their fateful journey with the Emerald. Apparently, the pair had swam down every waterway they could find on their way to Larkender Castle, calling upon friends to join them. Once arriving at Larkender Castle, the contingent of beavers had waited outside, submerged in the deep waters of the river until such time as they were needed. Both Kayden and Rosalyn had thanked them again.

"We would have drowned if not for you," Rosalyn had said with brimming eyes. The beavers stood on their hind legs, balancing themselves on their tails, and saluted before waddling down to the water's edge to search for a few tender saplings for lunch.

Next, Kayden spotted Randolph, Rosalyn's father, across the hall. He was engaged in animated conversation with a man carrying an armload of logs for the fire. Rosalyn had been thrilled to find her father among the Resistance fighters that had arrived on boats. He had been injured in the fighting on the other side of the river, as many had, but his wounds were not serious. In fact, thanks to the healing power of the Emerald, whirling in a dazzling green haze of light at the head of the sceptre, and held by King Larkender as he walked among the injured after the battle, all those who had been hurt were now fully recovered. Sadly, for those who had perished—whichever side they fought on—nothing could be done.

Not even the power of the Emerald could restore life when it was gone.

The king had even used the Emerald to heal those who had fought on the side of evil, although most of Respiele's soldiers had run for the hills when the war was over. Kayden supposed they were afraid of punishment, and hurried back to the familiar slopes of the Araleesh mountain range where they had dwelt for many years.

Kayden turned his gaze to his dear, hungry friend Talbot. Kayden grinned as the large figure paced toward a table laden with food. With a laugh, he wondered to himself if raspberry jam and toast had been provided, and if it had, would there ever be enough to satisfy the needs of the enormous hedgehog. Kayden's mind slipped back to the night before when they had talked together.

"Once I discovered you were gone, back in Norbern, I admit to panicking somewhat," Talbot had confided. He, Kayden, Rosalyn, Randolph, and the king all sat before a roaring fire in King Ludwig's private chambers. "Thankfully, Randolph found it, knew what sort of staff it was and brought it to me in Oglande after we parted in the forest," Talbot said with a nod to Kayden.

Talbot yawned and shifted his bulk into a more comfortable position as he sprawled over the width of a rug on the hearth. There was no chair that could hold him.

"In any case, I am grateful I could bring it to you," Talbot concluded. "You made good use of your Runestaff. Your grandmother would be proud. You have done a fine job, young man."

Kayden blushed, hoping in the fire's glow that no one would notice.

"Yes, glad I spotted it," Rosalyn's father interjected. The broad-shouldered man pushed himself forward on a plush red, velvet chair. "The Runestaff, that is. And I kept it safe, I did. I knew it had to belong to someone important, soon as I saw what it was."

He folded his arms across his chest and lifted his chin proudly.

"Indeed," Talbot said, acknowledging the man and the part he had played in their success. "We are most grateful to you, sir."

Kayden came back to the present and his gaze shifted to seek out Rosalyn's sleek black hair as she moved to and fro in the throng, speaking to all those she knew, which appeared to be almost everyone.

Rosalyn was amazing. Stories were circulating among the people of her bravery in battle. Talbot told him that during the time Kayden had stood, rooted to the spot as the battle was waged between Respiele and King Ludwig, she had fought off every foe that endeavored to attack Kayden from behind. Because of her, he was standing here today.

He watched as she stopped to exchange words with the leader of the Resistance, Sonalia. The two were quite similar, each of them strong, smart, and courageous. Sonalia had led her troops along the eastern road, arriving just in the nick of time to attack the closest flank of Respiele's forces.

Rosalyn, laughing with the leader over some shared joke, caught Kayden's eye across the room and lifted a hand to wave. He waved back and, saying goodbye to Sonalia, Rosalyn strode through the crowd toward him.

They were both given new clothes for the evening's festivities, and gazing at her, Kayden thought Rosalyn looked like a whole new person. She wore a long dress of a light, finely woven fabric, dyed a pale pink which suited her long, jet-black hair. Kayden could tell she didn't feel very happy in it, as she kept pulling at the puffed sleeves and tugging at the tight waist. He guessed she would have preferred her usual breeches, tunic, and cloak, but to him she looked beautiful.

"Hello," she said. "I am pleased to see you"

"I am pleased to see you too," he replied. "Will you sit with me?"

She nodded, a broad grin lighting up her face as she reached for his hand.

"We did it," she said.

Kayden squeezed her fingers and then laced them together with his own as she moved to stand next to him and look out upon the assembly.

The castle bustled with life and joy as tonight there would be a huge feast. A massive fire took up a portion of the wall along one side and light streamed in through gracefully curved, but narrow, windows down the other. Long tables lined the floor while men and women alike rushed between them carrying steaming dishes of food. At the far end of the enormous hall was a raised platform where King Larkender and Queen Mirabelle sat on large ornate chairs. In the corner near the monarchs, musicians with strange instruments played some of the oddest tunes Kayden had ever heard. The music was pleasing once he got used to it.

"Beggin' your pardon, sir," a young boy said, stopping in front of Kayden and ducking his head. "King Larkender wishes you both to seat yourselves at his table to eat. Will you follow me, please?"

Kayden shook off his reverie, and nodding, stepped out to follow him. Hand in hand, he and Rosalyn wove their way across the teeming floor. But as they walked, the way began to clear before them. The crowd grew quiet, stepping back to leave a wide space for him and Rosalyn to pass, and many heads bowed in acknowledgement.

Kayden didn't know what to do with all this attention. Embarrassed, he smiled at a few of the people. Though he mostly just focussed on the boy ahead of them, as the youngster led them to a table set just below the platform. The boy motioned to chairs where they should sit and Kayden pulled one out for Rosalyn before seating himself.

The entire room fell silent and all eyes looked expectantly at the king. Kayden and Rosalyn turned to watch him stand and move forward to address the hall.

The monarchs were not young. Their faces wore the trouble of many years and their hair was mainly silver, yet people lived much longer in Erinbourne it seemed. Besides, Kayden had seen the king in action and knew he was no doddering old man. Both wore richly coloured, thick purple robes, but beneath the splendor of the velvet, they had on simple clothes. Around the king's head was a narrow band of plated gold, rising to a solitary point over his forehead where a large opal was fixed into an intricate setting. Queen Mirabelle wore a similar circlet of gold that rested in hair artfully coiled upon her head. And, of course, King Larkender held the Golden Sceptre of Power.

The flashing lights of the Gemstones had since grown dim, but still, in the firelight of many torches set about the room, they gleamed with latent promise. Now that all four were present, King Larkender looked relaxed and at ease. The darkness had passed, and tonight was a time for merriment.

Behind and above the royal couple, long lengths of multi-coloured ribbons streamed, fixed and looping over their heads in the rafters in the high timbered ceiling. They were strung to honor the Gemstones of Power.

"A battle cannot be won alone," King Larkender began, in a voice that echoed throughout the great banquet hall. "It takes the strength and wisdom of the majority, the kingdom's people. Each individual must fight, in his or her own way, for the common good, and each deed, be it great or small, when combined together, ensures our victory."

He cleared his throat as though finding it difficult to continue. The room was deathly quiet.

"During these dark days I was, and am, proud of the sacrifice, determination, and unity each one of you demonstrated and of those who cannot be with us here tonight. I thank you for it. No one should ever be forced live in fear. Thankfully, the day of reckoning has arrived and Erinbourne is free once more." With this, he thrust the Golden Sceptre of Power high into the air.

The hall erupted in loud cheering. Hats were thrown into the air and the people jumped for joy.

He raised his other hand, asking for silence, and the room slowly settled.

"Now, let us eat, drink, and be merry!" he shouted.

With laughter and shouts of, "Long live King Larkender!" the room subsided into a happy clatter of dishes and scraping of chairs as each one sat to eat.

Kayden and Rosalyn, who had also stood to attention during the address, watched while the king offered an arm to his queen as she stepped from the platform.

"Sit, sit," King Ludwig said, waving for them to begin eating. "You must be hungry."

Rosalyn sat down and pulled a bowl of steaming vegetables toward her, but Kayden waited until the queen was seated before sliding into a chair near the king. As he began to fill his plate with the simple, delicious food, he noticed Sonalia and Talbot also making their way to the king's table and seating themselves on the other side of the monarch. Kayden was proud and happy. What a moment. Even in his wildest dreams he wouldn't have thought it could be this good.

Much later, he and Rosalyn leapt breathlessly onto the platform. Rosalyn had introduced him to all the Resistance fighters she knew, and they had danced until their feet hurt. Kayden's stomach muscles were sore with all the laughing they'd done as she tried to teach him the unusual dance steps that were popular in Erinbourne.

They plunked themselves on stools placed near the King, and with flushed faces watched people continue to whirl to the music and enjoy themselves.

Rosalyn went quiet. A curtain of hair hung across her face, obscuring her expression. She shifted uneasily and then turning to Kayden she flicked her dark curls away. Reaching out, she closed her hand over Kayden's where it rested on his knee.

"I am going to miss you Kayden from Canada," she whispered, looking up at him with glistening eyes. With the other hand she tucked her glossy tresses behind one ear. "I greatly enjoyed the journey... well, some of it at least." She laughed.

"You are so brave. So different from anyone I know," she said, removing her hand and sitting back in her chair again.

Kayden gazed at her in astonishment. Brave? Him? No one had ever said such a thing before. He sat up a little straighter.

"Same to you," he said quietly. "It sucks that I have to go. I'll never forget you."

She looked at him quizzically.

"I mean—I'm sad that I have to leave," he explained with a grin.

"Perhaps you shall come back one day," she asked hopefully, in the formal way the people of this land seemed to speak.

"That'd be cool," he said, leaning closer, and then moved back abruptly as Talbot mounted the stage to speak to them.

"We should be getting some rest," Talbot cautioned. "We leave for Durgot's tomorrow, and it will be early so I suggest you turn in soon. Good night, miss." His beady eyes flickered between them. Turning on his heel, he leapt from the platform, his long dangerous spines laid flat across his powerful back. Stopping to send them one last, measuring look, Talbot nodded and marched off through the laughing guests.

Kayden stood awkwardly to his feet.

"Goodnight King Larkender and Queen Mirabelle," he said, with a slight bow.

Rosalyn stood also and repeated the same farewell with a small curtsy.

The king looked kindly at them. His eyes crinkled up at the corners in a smile of both thanks and regret rolled into one.

"Good night to you both," he responded solemnly. Then, the great man stood to his feet and emphasized his next words. "This kingdom is in your debt, young sir and miss. We thank you most humbly."

To Kayden's astonishment, the king bowed low before them.

"Rosalyn," he continued, "you are deserving of great honour and your service shall be rewarded. I wish you to know that you and your father will be given all that you need to make your future lives prosperous, whatever that may entail. Also, should you wish to someday live within the walls of Larkender Castle as a knight, or in whatever capacity you may choose, it shall be accomplished with my blessing."

Rosalyn was clearly at a loss for words. She ducked her head and curtsied.

"Th-thank you," she stammered.

King Larkender shifted his gaze to Kayden and bushy brows met over his penetrating eyes.

"None of this," he said, flinging an arm to encompass the room and beyond into the world of Erinbourne, "would have been possible without you, son of Alainea Ilstyne and great grandson of Respiele Larkender. You were our only hope. And, in answering the call from a world beyond your own, you risked your own life to save not only my people, but an entire world from catastrophe. I hope you know how remarkable that sacrifice is."

He waited until Kayden nodded.

"Your commitment to aid this foreign land, to place yourself in danger for a people you did not hitherto know were kin, is highly commendable. You have shown great courage." King Ludwig lifted the gleaming sceptre. The jewels flickered in the firelight. "Remember, young nephew, that your presence here will one day be required again."

"I will remember," Kayden said gravely. "And thank you."

The king placed a hand on Kayden's shoulder before turning to help Queen Mirabelle to her feet. He then held up a hand for silence in the hall and a hush fell over the assembly.

"We owe a debt of gratitude to this young man and

woman," he announced in a booming voice. "Let us show our appreciation."

Throughout the hall, each person stood, lifted their hands high above their heads and began to clap. Feet stomped and voices rang out in praise as the room erupted with thunderous applause.

Kayden turned a deep shade of pink. He glanced at Rosalyn to see she had flushed crimson too. Then grinning, Kayden leaped into the air with a whoop and swung his fist in the air.

This was a moment he would remember for the rest of his life. It was perfect. A perfect end to the craziest adventure imaginable.

Chapter Fifteen

The next morning, Kayden and Talbot stood just inside the castle gates, ready to leave. A tall, sorrel mare patiently waited nearby, laden with supplies needed to see them safely back to the door between their worlds.

A large group had arrived to see them off. Even Merlot, the stiyaha who had helped them to escape, had appeared from the dense forest near the river. He stood at the dark edge of trees, lifting an arm of farewell before disappearing back into the leafy glade.

The king and queen expressed their gratitude yet again and said their goodbyes. Before Kayden left, however, the king motioned that he step to one side for a private chat.

"Malahd does not issue idle threats," King Ludwig said, laying both hands on Kayden's shoulders. "I am sure that, before long, he will return for vengeance. You must be prepared."

Kayden cleared his throat. "You think Malahd will come after *me* in Canada, like he did to find the Emerald? But why?"

"Because you were the key reason he was defeated," the king said. "Your ability to carry the Emerald and wield the Runestaff threatens him. Because he is malicious, blood-thirsty, and cruel, and will not stop in his evil pursuit until either he, or we are destroyed." King Ludwig exhaled. "And because you, as my only living relative, are heir to the throne of Erinbourne. Malahd's ultimate goal is to rule this kingdom. You and I stand in the way of his twisted desires." The man dropped his hands and searched Kayden's eyes.

Kayden looked away. All this talk of him being next in line to the throne was upsetting. "What do you want me to do?" he asked.

"It will take time for Malahd to recover from this blow. But he will. I want you to be vigilant. Never let down your guard and, when the time is right, return to us. Whether you knew of your heritage before this point, you know it now. Your destiny lies in Erinbourne. When trouble next assails the people of this land, you will not require someone to seek you out and ask you to come to our aid, as happened the first time. You will perceive the summons yourself. Here." King Larkender lightly placed his fingertips over Kayden's heart.

Kayden didn't know what to say. It was a lot to process. He was filled with concern for his friends when, as King Ludwig said, Malahd returned. But for now he wasn't ready to accept the truth that pointed to his inheritance.

"I wish you a safe journey back to your family Kayden." The king smiled, still looking worried as he moved away. "One day soon we shall meet again."

"Thanks, I'll remember what you've said." Kayden walked to the horse, a sudden rush of emotion causing him to scan the crowd for Rosalyn. The thought that he should stay ran through his mind. In a short space of time, he'd come to care about this land, and its inhabitants. But he would be back, that much he knew for sure.

Talbot had returned to his diminutive size and peeked out of as old canvas bag as Kayden swung it over his back and settled himself onto the horse. His eyes found Rosalyn in the crowd. She stood beside her father, looking sad. Kayden waved at her one last time, lingering, before he urged the horse to trot through the massive gates and down the cobblestones to cross the bridge.

And so, he and Talbot began their journey home.

King Ludwig had offered a fancy carriage with horses and men to drive them home in style. Instead, Kayden preferred to spend the time alone with the small hedgehog who had become his friend and protector, just as Durgot had predicted.

This time it was an easy trip. They were relaxed, making their way back to Durgot's home beneath the mountain without incident. And since a proper tent had been furnished for the journey, they were comfortable. At Kayden's request, they stopped for a short visit with the beavers, Camden and Edna, even though Kayden was anxious to get home.

Passing alongside sun-lit fields of grain, his thoughts rested on his family and the rolling landscape of the farm. And Gran! The stories they would have to share when she and Kayden had time alone. He wondered what had happened since his hasty departure and if time had really allowed him to be gone so many days without being missed. He even thought of his little sister Sarah. She could be annoying, but he loved her.

Before Kayden knew it, they'd recovered Durgot's small boat from Camden, and were manoeuvering it back along the Enchanted River that encircled the interior of the

Ildune Mountain. Kayden laid his oar on the bottom of the craft and rested his hands on the sides. There was nothing to do now but wait for the current to carry them to Durgot's door.

The clammy, cold, darkness was not frightening this time. Kayden eagerly stared at the steep walls of the mountain rearing up beside him as they floated along, watching for signs of the portal that would mark the beginning of his exit from this world and entrance into his own.

Finally, he saw the door high above him in the rock. Using caution, he and Talbot jumped onto the narrow shelf and pulled the boat up on the craggy ledge to dry. Kayden withdrew the boussole from his pants pocket and slid a thumb over its polished surface. Lifting his faithful staff, he smiled in acknowledgement at the silvery likeness indented into the wood, before touching it to the slot that appeared in the stone wall. Familiar steps slid into view. He and Talbot mounted them quickly. They stepped to the massive stone door, awaiting the Gatekeeper.

And he was there. Ever vigilant at his post, Durgot had known of their arrival and the great door swung wide on silent hinges. The little man in the billowing blue suit and hat stood in the gap, grinning as he ushered them inside. After shutting the door behind them with a soft click, Durgot flung his arms around Kayden, knocking the wide-brimmed cap from his greying head in the process. Laughing, Kayden ran to fetch it from under some shrubs where it had rolled and placed it back upon Durgot's head.

"I am absolutely ecstatic to welcome you back!" Durgot said.

They didn't speak another word as they crossed the beautiful gardens to Durgot's house, but the gatekeeper danced before them with barely suppressed excitement as they walked. It was late morning on the fifteenth day of Kayden's adventure, and they climbed the vast number of stairs, thankful to arrive at the canary-yellow door. Hurrying ahead of them, Durgot flung it open and graciously ushered them inside with a bow.

"Young sir, young sir!" Durgot repeated, his beard bobbing up and down and his large floppy hat almost flying off again as he nodded vigorously. "My heart overflows with gladness."

With quick steps, he led them into his bright comfortable kitchen. "I bid you rest yourselves. It is with the utmost gratification I witness your presence before me. The sun fairly radiates with renewal since you completed your quest and I..."

Kayden interrupted, "You're doing it again." He held up a hand in weak protest, then placed the man's silver boussole on the worn old table. "I think you're happy we're back, but it's a little hard to tell."

Talbot laughed as he hopped onto a chair and looked around for something to eat.

"Speak plainly and dish out the raspberry jam," he said with a chuckle, his eyes glittering with mirth. "We shall tell all once we have eaten."

Long into the afternoon they relayed their adventures amid endless rounds of toast, several jars of glistening red jam, and mugs of steaming tea. At last, Durgot stood and placed a hand on Kayden's shoulder.

"My dear young man, it draws near to the hour in which you must depart. We cannot allow your parents to worry. Much as I would like for you to spend time with me here, it is with sadness I must see you through my gate, and into your world once more."

The now somber trio walked quietly together toward

the portal built into the mountainside, their laughter giving way to thoughts of the farewell that lay ahead. Kayden looked back over his shoulder at the thin red dwelling behind him and wondered when he would see it or these two friends again. Erinbourne and its people had become pivotal points of change in his life. He knew without a doubt he was not the same young man who had arrived at Durgot's house a few short days ago. He turned back to walk the dusty path under the mountain with a smile. Deep within, he knew he would be back in Erinbourne soon.

Together, they passed through the gate and with the help of Durgot's staff, safely crossed the black waters of the River Enchanted. Trudging up the uneven rock path toward the final exit back to his grandmother's land, Kayden's steps slowed.

"I'm gonna miss you guys," Kayden finally said, his voice barely above a whisper. "Thanks for everything."

"Do you mean to say you are thanking us for involving you in a scheme that could have ended in your untimely death or possible dismemberment?" Talbot asked from where he was riding in Kayden's backpack.

"Yeah," Kayden answered with a chuckle. "That's exactly what I'm thanking you for."

They stopped in the tiny chamber that Kayden recalled from that first night within the mountain after escaping the insidious purple fog. In the wavering light of the staff he carried, Kayden thought he saw a tear trickle down Durgot's grizzled cheeks and disappear into his grey beard.

"As I mentioned once before," Durgot said, his words measured and clear, "you are much like your esteemed grandfather and I am proud to know you, young man."

He grasped Kayden's hands. "Please give my fondest regards to Alainea." His voice trembled. Now Kayden was certain that Durgot's eyes had welled up with tears. "Please tell her for me that her grandson's bravery and willingness to help us will never be forgotten."

Sniffling, Durgot felt for the correct spot along the wall, raised his weathered old Runestaff, and struck a resounding blow.

The fissure appeared with a loud cracking noise and spread apart to reveal the forest outside and beyond that, the fields that Kayden knew so well. Removing his pack, he set it carefully on the ground. Talbot leapt out and eyed him gravely.

"Farewell, until we meet again, Kayden," he said. "Never forget who you are—the heir of Erinbourne."

He sat up on his hind legs and held a paw in the air as he fixed Kayden with a hard stare. "And remember the lessons you have learned beyond our gates. Lesson number three: One courageous act can change the world."

The fracture in the rock was closing. Kayden stepped through and turned to watch the faces of his friends blur, melting into the gloom that was within the mountain. Then, with a mighty crash, the crevice closed and Kayden stood staring up at the sheer rock face, alone in the shadow of Alberta's Rocky Mountains.

Chapter Sixteen

Kayden's arrival home had been distinctly anti-climactic. After picking his way back across rocks, through dense forest, and trudging across the freshly combined fields near his home, he'd tramped up the old wooden steps to the farmhouse, and in through the screen door without anyone even asking where he'd been. It was bizarre.

Even more bizarre—he'd returned in time for supper, and his boisterous family had gathered at the dining table that night to discuss Gran's amazing recovery. She was fine. It was wonderful to hear she would be back home again.

"Furthermore…" Kayden's dad announced, "your mother and I have talked, and we believe our lives have all been changed for the better by moving here. Sure, we've had to work a little harder, and make some sacrifices. But all that should settle down once we get the ranch operating smoothly. So…we're going to remain on the ranch with Gran."

Kayden cheered along with his sister, and his dad sighed

with relief. At one time, Kayden reflected, to be told that he must stay on the ranch forever would have felt like a life sentence, whereas now it was great news.

The next day, Kayden and his family drove to town in a high state of excitement. Gran was coming home. Although it raised a few questions, Kayden had insisted he take along Gran's old grey staff.

"It'll help her walk," he'd explained, fitting it into the car with difficulty.

She was waiting on a bench in the front hall looking out the window when they arrived.

Kayden was the first to spot his grandmother, but stood back as everyone rushed to hug her and convince themselves she was really okay. Gran held Kayden's mom and dad tightly and then her eyes met Kayden's over Sarah's head as the girl threw her arms around her grandmother. Gran cast Kayden an inquisitive look, and he gave her a convincing smile. However, as Kayden held the door for her to proceed his family outside, her gaze flickered to the long grey staff leaning against the car. She shot him another glance.

"I brought your staff for you, Gran," Kayden stated, his face lighting up with happiness to see his beloved grandmother looking so well. "Thought you could use it to lean on."

She settled herself in the front seat, shrugging off all offers of assistance.

"No, thank you dear. I shall be just fine," she said. "It belongs to you now, Kayden. I imagine you have likely earned it these past few days."

The family cast one another questioning looks at this mysterious remark as they motored down city streets on their way back to the farm. Kayden reached forward to rest a hand lovingly on his grandmother's shoulder. He could hardly wait to talk to her alone.

———————

Early Monday morning, the alarm clock beside Kayden's bed startled him into awareness. He rolled over and groaned, but fear of the day ahead was not the reason why. He simply didn't feel like getting up.

Dragging on his usual jeans and plaid shirt, he yawned and reached for his Runestaff. Good thing his parents weren't around to question him. As long as the bus driver allowed it, the Runestaff was going to school with him today. He couldn't be sure it would respond to him in the same way here as it had in Erinbourne, but even if it didn't he refused to back down from bullies ever again, and if it did—he had plans.

He flew up the steps of the school bus with a cheery greeting for the driver. If the retired farmer wondered why Kayden was carrying an oddly patterned stick, he didn't ask, but he did stop Kayden with a look of both concern and relief.

"I hear your grandmother made a full recovery," the man began with a nod as he put the vehicle into gear. "I'm real glad to hear it."

He paused. "Don't you think you should sit a little closer to the front?"

Kayden realized the man was worried for his safety.

"I'll be fine, Mr. McLean," he said, and moved to his usual seat at the back of the bus.

As if on cue, one of the sneering boys, Kaleb, who hung around with Dillon, jammed his foot into the aisle in front of Kayden. Lightly, Kayden hopped over the sneakered foot and flung himself into his seat to stare out the window with a smile.

I've dealt with a lot worse stuff than these guys, he thought, standing the staff up beside him and holding it so it wouldn't tumble over.

Two seats back, Hudson raised himself up, hoisting a heavy binder over Kayden's head.

"Sit down!" the driver yelled from behind the wheel, glancing into the mirror above him. "I'm watching you."

With a glare for the older man, Hudson retreated back into his seat, but the group talked quietly among themselves for the duration of the ride to school.

When the bus pulled up before the school, Kayden was up and out the door. It didn't take a rocket scientist to know his tormentors would be planning something painful for him if he hung around. Hurrying onto the lawn in front of the imposing brick building, Kayden looked for Matt, the friend he'd made at school on Friday, before he'd left for Erinbourne. Had it only been two days ago that they'd spoken? Seemed like a year.

Spotting Matt on the school steps with a book open on his lap, Kayden sprinted down the sidewalk.

"Hey Matt, how was your weekend?" Kayden skidded to a halt and plunked himself down on the cement.

Matt peered at him through thick glasses and a smile broke over his face as he closed the book with a snap and faced Kayden.

"It was okay. Nothing special. How about yours?" he asked. Then, peering over Kayden's shoulder, he said, "Don't look now, but Dillon and his friends are coming. We gotta get out of here."

He jumped up and scurried into the school.

Kayden charged after him.

"Listen Matt," Kayden said, and then grabbed Matt's arm as the heavy glass doors swung closed, protecting them for now. "I want to talk to you about that. We can't live in fear any longer. Something has to be done and I plan to do it today…"

───────────

Kayden knew it was only a matter of time before he had to face the bigger boys and he wanted to do it on his own terms. He was sick of letting them dictate his life and saw the fear they had instilled in other kids too. Someone had to do something.

Seeing Dillon in the hallway between classes, he strode over to him.

"Dillon," he said, gathering his courage. "You want to pound my face in, right?"

A disbelieving smirk spread across Dillon's face as he nodded.

"Great," Kayden continued. He spoke with more bravery than he felt. "Then meet me at the ball diamond behind the school at twelve."

Dillon motioned for a buddy to step closer. "Just listen to this stupid kid," he said. "He's offering to be beaten up. Text the others and tell them to meet us at the ball diamond at noon."

The pair laughed. "Make sure you show up, you little jerk. I'm looking forward to this." Dillon reached out to shove Kayden into a locker with a noise that caused kids passing by to stop and take a different route. Then, he turned on his heel and stalked away.

Kayden straightened himself up amid curious stares,

rounded a corner and flopped against a locker, breathing heavily. *Am I crazy?* Weakly, he shifted himself upright and taking a firm grip on his binder, pushed open the door to science class where he tried without success to concentrate on the lesson.

The bell rang for lunch. Chattering kids poured out of their classrooms and spilled into the hallway. In seconds, Kayden was the only one left in the room. Still, he lingered at his desk, closing his books, and stuffing a pencil into his shirt pocket before sliding out to stand. Walking sightlessly to his locker, he stowed everything inside, then looked around for Matt, but his friend was nowhere to be seen.

Just as well. If this ends badly, I don't want him getting hurt too.

Kayden strode to the opposite end of the school and, checking that no one was watching, ducked into a small closet-like room where the janitor kept brooms, mops, and other items to clean the school. Reaching among the long handles, he withdrew his staff from the spot where he had hidden it earlier that morning. He looked at it a long moment, then straightened his shoulders and marched out the back doors toward the baseball diamonds.

Ten or eleven older teens, friends of Dillon, were milling in an angry mob around the side of a game shed where equipment was kept during the warm months of the year. Kayden took a deep breath, clutched his staff tighter, and held his head high as he marched into view. When he was only a few meters away from Dillon, he stopped.

"Aw look, the baby brought an itty-bitty stick to play with?" Dillon said. "You're makin' this way too easy."

He looked around at the boys who stood with him. They

sniggered and elbowed one another as though they could hardly wait for the fun to begin.

"Can you believe this guy?" Dillon asked, rolling his eyes for the benefit of the crowd. He jerked a thumb at Kayden and laughed.

Then, snarling an obscenity, Dillon pulled something out of his pocket and flipped open the blade of a long, deadly looking knife. Dillon's friends gathered in closer, silently watching their fearless leader. Several of them even got out their phones to take videos.

"I don't want to fight you," Kayden said, ignoring Dillons threatening stance, "but I do want you to quit scaring the kids at this school. So, I guess I'll have to stop you—and your friends."

He glanced around at the hostile faces in front of him.

A couple of the bigger boys, Karl and Jake, imitated his words in a high falsetto. "Oooh, I guess I'll have to stop you."

Everyone laughed and jostled each other as they too imitated Kayden.

"Like, we're so scared," Jake said, moving forward to take a poke at Kayden. Several others did the same. Kayden stepped back as each swipe came a little closer to his body. Soon, they'd connect. He kept his eyes focussed, however, on Dillon.

Dillon lunged forward, slashing at Kayden with a practised move. But Kayden was faster. Bringing the staff down in front of his face with both hands, he drove it into the dirt with an ominous thud where, gyrating madly, it became a whirling grey blur, exploding into a snarling grey wolf that landed in a cloud of dust before the startled eyes of the gang. It planted huge paws firmly in Dillon's path and fixed him with gleaming black eyes. Its ears were laid, flat to its head, and from somewhere deep in its chest, it growled menacingly past an upper lip that curled over long jagged teeth and slavering jaws.

Leaping backward, Dillon cowered with a muffled oath, throwing his hands over his head for protection. Amid screams from the assembled boys, and the sound of phones dropping to earth, the wolf sprang, its powerful muscles coiling and jaws snapping shut just shy of Dillon's jugular. Dillon tumbled to the ground whimpering. Then, the monstrous beast whirled up into the air, and flew back to become, once again, nothing more than a humble grey stick —resting on the ground—held by Kayden.

As Dillon strove to regain his breath, his chest heaving, his eyes glazed with fear, Kayden heard footsteps behind him. The bully snapped his head up to look at what fresh horror this kid might hold in his hands, and his friends turned their panicked gaze to the area behind Kayden.

At first it was only a few kids that appeared around the corner of the building behind Matt. They stopped beside Kayden, eyeing Dillon and the gang of boys who had terrorized their school for too long. And then more kids marched up to stand wordlessly in solidarity. Soon, the baseball diamond was filled with kids young and old, girls and boys, of all shapes and sizes. And still they continued to come, silently, lending their support, laying down the law, joining together as one.

Kayden's face glowed, and his heart burst with happiness at this show of support from the students at school that only last week he had hated with a passion.

"You see, Dillon," Kayden said, turning back to the boy, "this is called the strength of the majority. You and your friends will *not* bully kids in this school any longer or you'll have every one of us to deal with." He leaned closer. "And my friend here too."

He brought the staff down on the ground for emphasis. Dillon shrieked and scrambled backward through the dirt in an attempt to put distance between himself and the slender grey staff.

Matt grinned at Kayden, pushing his ever-sliding glasses higher up on his nose, and then the two friends turned, melting into the crowd behind them as everyone made their way back into the school for lunch.

It wasn't until Kayden was riding home on the bus that afternoon that he thought of it. Dillon and his two friends had been quite subdued in the back of the vehicle, warily watching Kayden as he found his seat and settled into it with his Runestaff. Kayden paid them no notice at all. He stared out the window beside him at the craggy blue peaks of the Rocky Mountains and sighed with contentment. Life was good.

"Lesson number four," he whispered to himself with a smile. "A battle cannot be won by just one person. It takes all people, working together, to win the war."

Kayden looked down at the seatback in front of him as a sudden vision flooded his mind. He saw Malahd vanishing in a cloud of swirling black mist and heard his high-pitched scream as he swore to kill the king—and him. Kayden shivered. Then he thought of his final exchange with King Larkender. The king himself had said that Kayden's destiny lay in Erinbourne. Maybe it was true. A part of his soul existed in both worlds now, and he missed the hidden land beyond the mountain portal, a lot.

His gaze flickered back outside. He would be watchful for evil on the horizon, as King Larkender had stressed he should, and Kayden knew he would go back one day to help fight the epic battle that was yet to come. But this time, he'd be ready.

Kayden closed his eyes. He rested his head on the seat and dreamt of the far-away land of Erinbourne, and of a very dangerous girl.

vinci-books.com/thelegacy

Destiny awakens in the shadows of a forgotten birthright.

Fueled by vengeance, Kayden seeks the sorcerer who destroyed his family and stole the realm's deadliest weapon. But as he braves treacherous lairs and monstrous foes, he uncovers a hidden birthright that may hold the key to saving Erinbourne. Can he unlock its power before darkness consumes the land?

Turn the page for a free preview…

The Legacy: Chapter One

"The reign of Erinbourne's king must end, and his line be destroyed," Malahd said with a snarl. "It is well he has no offspring to deal with. Before the full moon wanes, King Larkender will be dead, and *I* shall possess the Gemstones of Erinbourne."

An unwilling sunbeam slanted through the narrow window of the great dining hall in Respiele's forgotten fortress. Two torches burned on either side of a massive oaken door, and by this light, the occupants talked. Snurler, captain of the stronghold's small group of defenders, sat twisting his hands together at a long table recently cleared of some meager meal. Malahd, the sorcerer, paced nearby, his feet making no sound as he moved along the cold flagstones.

He whirled about at the far end of the room. His long black robe swished around his ankles as he paused. He struck the flagstones with the end of a long silver staff to punctuate his remark with barely suppressed glee. Red sparks burst from the tip, illuminating the sorcerer's stringy grey hair, and crooked smile distorted by hatred. Malahd held the smooth rod in his one good hand. The other was not a hand at all, but a gleaming metal claw. He glided back.

"Larkender is a fool. He has no more idea how to wield the power of the sceptre, and its gemstones, than that of an infant." Malahd stopped beside Snurler. "Too long have I waited to rule this land."

Spittle flew from his thin lips with his angry pronouncement. Snurler watched in alarm as the saliva landed on his sleeve with a puff of smoke, singeing a hole in the rough cloth.

"Yes, sir." Snurler crouched a little lower on his stool, surreptitiously wiping his arm down one leg of his breeches. "But are you not forgetting the other—"

Malahd flung himself at Snurler.

"Forget? You fool! I assure you nothing escapes my memory or intellect!" He banged a fist onto the wood beside Snurler's face, sending crumbs bouncing. "What are you saying? Be out with it!"

Snurler opened his mouth and then slammed it shut just as quick. Shifting uncomfortably on the stool, he drew his tattered cloak closer around his thin frame and opened his mouth to speak again. Still, he said nothing.

Snurler's eyes flicked into the dim recesses of the room where a small movement had captured his eye, but it was only a mouse. Malahd always made sure he and Snurler were alone for these conversations. If the sorcerer chose to punish the captain, there would be no one to object.

In any case, no one *would* object to anything Malahd said or did, if they knew what was good for them. People had been killed for less than what Snurler was about to say now. Yet after years of servitude to this cruel master with nothing to show for it except the misery of his body and soul, some part of Snurler wanted to see the sorcerer squirm.

"There...there is one other of Larkender lineage," Snurler said. "Remember the boy who carried the Emerald? I have heard he is grandson of Alainea Ilstyne, one of the ancient Garde of these Araleesh Mountains, and the great-grandson of Respiele Larkender himself."

Snurler ducked his head beneath the strong wooden table beside him in anticipation of the blow that would follow this foul reminder. Yet, he spoke again, his voice thin and wobbly. "You know, as well as I, that if it is true, the boy is heir to the throne of Erinbourne."

With a hiss of rage, Malahd swung his staff through the air, an arc of tiny red coals following the movement. The embers flew high, crackling and snapping, before dropping onto Snurler's unprotected head. The coals sizzled there, filling the room with a choking smell of burning hair and flesh. Then, the sorcerer pointed the tip of his staff, and a ribbon of fire leapt from the silver tip to where Snurler crouched, batting at his head in a frantic effort to rid himself of the smouldering embers. Weaving about the captain's body, Malahd's curling threads of flame lifted Snurler, screaming, into the smoky air.

"You dare to speak to me of this illegitimate child! We have no proof the boy is Respiele's descendant." Malahd extended his arm a little further, slamming Snurler against a spot on the wall near the ceiling. He held him there within a living inferno. "A mere child cannot defeat *me*."

Malahd drew himself up to his full height. "Besides, this...boy returned to his own kind long ago, through the portal that divides our worlds. He cannot return to Erinbourne without aid, and the ill plans I have arranged for the king are known only by me. There is no one to prevent the actions of such a powerful sorcerer as myself." Malahd jabbed the staff toward the helpless Snurler again. "Do you hear? No one! Every inhabitant of this land shall fear me and bow to my desires!"

A liquid blue flame ran from Malahd's staff, merging with the ruby red, and mutating into deepening threads of cobalt. It licked at Snurler's face. Fingers of indigo fire crept about his chest and legs, pinning him to the scored rock wall. The blue blaze lit his eyes with a turquoise terror. Yet it did not burn him, and he slumped against the raging inferno knowing escape useless, but hoping his words might have some effect.

"Release me," Snurler croaked. "Have I served you all these many years to be treated thus? Someone had to remind you. The boy was here once—perhaps he could traverse through the great portal again."

Snurler took a ragged breath, needing to finish the task he had set before himself, despite his own peril.

Malahd relaxed his grip and Snurler slid down the stony wall, his body jolting over the rough surface. Then, impatiently, the sorcerer turned away, lowering his staff, and the blue flame thinned and returned like the thong of a whip to its owner. Snurler dropped to the ground with a sickening crunch and a scream of pain.

Furiously, Malahd marched along one side of the long table, ignoring the gurgling moans that issued from Snurler's crumpled form.

With his tongue, Snurler pushed a mouthful of blood and teeth onto the floor. His suffering at the hands of Malahd would be over soon, and part of him was relieved. Gathering himself for one last declaration, Snurler drew a tiny, rasping breath. He was past feeling fear. Loathing for the tyrant curled in his stomach, and he wished only to inject as much doubt as possible into the heart of the sorcerer he had both served and despised. Unable to move, his body wracked with pain, Snurler spoke from the floor.

"R-remember this—if the boy—does return..." he rasped, stuttering with pain. He paused to take a small bubbling breath, "and if he seeks you out—know that he will find—more of his inheritance—beneath this mountain than he or anyone else alive—could ever dream of."

Snurler's wasted body spasmed. "...A-and if he finds that inheritance, *you* are the one who should be afraid."

Malahd rounded on Snurler to finish him, aiming a bolt of jagged fire at the crushed remains, but all breath was gone from the broken body. The empty shell that once was Snurler, finally lay at rest. Malahd could inflict nothing more upon the man.

In a shadowed corner of the room, the little mouse dropped to all fours before it scurried through an opening in the rock and was gone.

Malahd shrieked with fury. Flinging his cloak behind his shoulders, he lifted his staff and ground it with all his might into the rock beneath his feet. Fire fell around him like blood-soaked rain from the rafters. The mountain that he stood upon rumbled from somewhere far, far below.

The Legacy: Chapter Two

Kayden pulled the uncomfortable bowtie from around his neck. He tossed it onto his bed before shrugging out of his suit jacket and hanging it carefully over a chair. He'd done it —graduated from high school. Resting his hands on the ancient wooden bureau that had been in this room since his father was a kid, Kayden leaned over the littered surface and searched the face reflected in the ornate mirror hanging above. He'd changed quite a bit in the three years since his family had moved to his grandparents' ranch in Southern Alberta.

He'd lost that perpetual look of fear he'd worn back then, and thought he even had an air of confidence about him now. Long gone was the former anxiety of his new life and school. He no longer wanted to return to his old life in Toronto. He'd enjoyed his senior year at school and loved country living.

He stared into the yellow eyes that he and his grand-mother shared and ran fingers through his ginger hair as he straightened. In fact, a lot of the kids looked up to him like he was some kind of hero after the day he'd taken his runestaff to school and dealt with the group that had terrorized his high school. Once he and a group of teenagers stood up to the bullies, all the students breathed easier. There was strength in numbers, and of course, in his magical runestaff.

That was the last time the staff had responded to him in any great capacity. Gran had told him the runestaff wouldn't be able to do much of significance here because it drew its energy from Erinbourne. Now, in Canada, it simply leaned in a corner of his closet. Yet, he thought about the magical staff and his friends in Erinbourne every day.

He turned away from the mirror to finish undressing and hang the rented suit back in its carrying bag. Then, he slid on a pair of well-worn jeans and a t-shirt, tucked his cell phone into a back pocket, and hurried downstairs.

"You're not going to a grad party tonight?" his father asked, as Kayden plopped onto a chair at the kitchen table beside him and poured a glass of iced tea.

The family had come home right after final ceremonies. Gran, his sister Sarah, and his mother were still upstairs changing.

"Nope, I have better things to do." Kayden grinned at his father's surprised expression. "I need to pack and get a good night's sleep, because…if you're okay with it, I want to take a couple days and go hiking into the mountains. I'll be careful."

His father laughed. "That's fine with me. Your mother might disagree. But if that's how my eighteen-year-old wants to celebrate his graduation, I think it's great." He clapped Kayden on the shoulder and held up his glass to clink. "Congratulations, son. I'm proud of you. I know it wasn't easy to move here and start a new school and life, but you did it, and did it well."

"Thanks, Dad." Kayden flushed with pride

It surprised him that his parents had known the difficulties he had when they first moved to the ranch. He'd hated it here then. But after meeting Durgot, the little man who was gatekeeper of the portal between Kayden's world and the alternate universe of Erinbourne, and carrying the powerful Emerald to its king, Kayden had returned a changed person. It had been an amazing adventure. And it was to Erinbourne that he planned to travel now. Of course, he couldn't say that since only Gran knew of its existence.

Fortunately, time passed differently in Erinbourne. If he allowed himself two days to be gone on this side of the portal, he should have ample time to cross through the divide and visit the people he cared about. As long as he could figure out how to do it. He longed to go back, especially to see Rosalyn.

Kayden got up from the table and set his glass in the sink. He knew it was more than just missing his friends. Lately, he'd begun to feel Erinbourne pulling him, as though he were being called from the other side. He placed a hand on his chest and remembered when King Ludwig had done the same. That great man had made it clear that Kayden would know in his heart, when it was time to return.

"I'm gonna get packed then," he said. Coming to stand beside his father he asked in an undertone, "Will you break it to mom for me?"

"I'll tell her and Gran when they get back," his dad said with a smile. "The pup tent is on a shelf behind my old golf clubs, and I think all the sleeping bags are there too."

Scraping his chair away from the table, he stood, and threw an arm around Kayden's shoulders as they walked to the basement door. "You'll take your bow?"

Once Kayden had turned sixteen and gotten his driver's license, he'd been quick to join the local archery club and begin learning the art.

"Definitely." He left his dad standing at the top of the stairs and clattered hurriedly down to the cement floor below.

Kayden deliberated over what to take with him. The last time he'd passed through the portal he hadn't known what to expect. This time he would be a little more prepared. He grabbed his sleeping bag and fastened it and the small tent to straps that hung from a large backpack. Then he searched for the kit he'd assembled for a school photography trip: tiny frying pan, razor-sharp pocketknife, matches, spoon, first aid stuff, a flashlight, and a lightweight thermos. Shrugging the laden bag onto his shoulders, he clumped upstairs to find the rest of his family assembled in the kitchen.

"Hi," he said, glancing nervously at his mother, who was rinsing a bowl of fruit at the sink. He swung the pack off his back and dumped it onto the floor, bracing himself for her lecture on safety and not going out alone. She dried her hands on a towel and walked toward him.

"Have a good time honey," she said. Reaching up, she held his face and looked lovingly into his eyes before pulling him down to plant a kiss on his cheek. Her eyes glistened. "I was so proud of you today. When you get home, I'll have a special supper for you. All your favourites."

Sniffling, she tucked a strand of light brown hair behind her ear. She stepped back to pull a tissue from a box on the counter and dab at her eyes.

Gran spoke from her seated position at the table. "We're all proud as punch of the young man you've become, Kayden."

Her face was wreathed in smiles.

"Yeah, even me," Sarah said, poking her head around the corner. "Surprised?" she added, making a face at him.

Chuckling, she disappeared into the living room with her book.

"Thanks a lot. You guys mean the world to me." Kayden stepped around the backpack and whisked his mother into his arms, swinging her off her feet.

"Stop!" she said, giggling. "Do you want to break your back before you leave?"

Setting her down gently, he moved to Gran. Leaning over the elderly woman, he enveloped her in a hug too.

"You're the best family anyone could ask for," Kayden said. He turned quickly before they saw the tears in his eyes. He walked into the kitchen where he opened cupboard doors, removed a few food items like cookies, bread, and peanut butter, and began to prepare some sandwiches.

Later, back in his room, he stuffed extra socks and underwear inside the bag, then stepped to his closet to rummage around at the bottom for the things he'd worn last time he'd been in Erinbourne. Pulling them out, he held up the old-fashioned breeches. They were way too small for him now and he folded them back up. Same with the boots and tunic he'd been given at the Resistance camp so long ago.

The only thing he might take was the cloak, although it would be short. He wanted to fit in with what others were wearing once he got there and not stand out, but he guessed he'd figure out how to do that when the time came. He threw the cloak behind him on the bed to be included.

After laying the other things he'd outgrown carefully inside his closet on a shelf, he reached into the corner for the most important item of all—his runestaff. Pushing aside hangers, he grasped the walking staff that was so much more than what it appeared. It was lightweight, grey in colour, and looked rather unremarkable, but he knew what wonders it was capable of.

He could hardly wait to use it again. He ran his fingers over the images etched from top to bottom along its length. The bed creaked as he moved to sit at one end, holding the runestaff before him and studying each carving.

There was a slight tap at the door.

"Come in."

Gran's grey head appeared in the light of the hallway and Kayden beckoned to her.

"I've been expecting you," he said, patting a spot beside him.

Her eyes flew to the runestaff and then to Kayden before she perched on the bed.

"I was going to make sure you took it along," she said quietly, nodding at the staff. "I know where you are going, my dear, and I wish you a safe journey."

"I thought you'd guess." He smiled at her. His heart warmed, thinking of the common bond they shared.

She reached for his hand and squeezed it tight.

"Please greet them all for me, will you? Especially Durgot and Talbot." Her yellow eyes shone in the light from a lamp on his bedside table. "There are times when I wish I could go back. If Dranich were alive…"

Her voice broke off and then she patted Kayden's knee and said briskly, "But I have my memories to hold onto and I have my family here." She smiled and looked away. "We were quite a pair, Dranich and I. There was nothing we could not do together. I only wish you could have experienced it, my boy."

She sighed deeply.

"You mean—riding a dragon?" Kayden asked hesitantly.

"In part. But mostly I refer to the closeness we shared. We knew one another's thoughts almost before they were thoughts at all. It was a dreadful day when dragons were erased from Erinbourne. It would have been your birthright to be united with such a mighty creature," she added. "And as future king, you would have been powerful indeed."

"Gran. Don't say that. I'm no king," Kayden said. He looked down and brushed imaginary lint from his jeans. "I understand about the bloodlines and everything, but it's crazy to think that *I* could be a king."

"Ah," she said, her eyes twinkling at him, "yet such decisions are not our own. We may neither choose nor decline what fate decrees. There is a reason for everything under the sun and this may well be your destiny, as it was mine to come to Canada. I believe you were destined to be in Erinbourne the last time. Do *you* not?"

She raised her eyebrows, daring him to disagree.

"Yeah, I know you're right. I think I was meant to play a part in saving Erinbourne and King Larkender."

"Your great-uncle," Gran said.

"Yes," he answered. "My great-uncle. But I still don't see how I could ever be a king."

After his grandmother had kissed him goodbye and tiptoed from the room, Kayden's thoughts lingered on what Gran had said about her dragon.

"It would have been great," he said to himself. Closing

his eyes, he could see it—a huge golden dragon coiled with massive wings outstretched as it poised on a mountain peak. He yearned for what could have been, but brought his thoughts back to the present, and the urgency he felt within. He was being summoned, but for what reason, he did not know.

The Legacy: Chapter Three

Kayden woke before sunrise. In fact, he had barely slept at all, so great was his excitement. Flipping on the lamp, he dressed without a sound, grabbed his runestaff and backpack, and eased down the staircase to the kitchen below.

His stomach was in too much turmoil to eat. Instead, he filled his thermos with cold water, grabbed an apple, and two granola bars to jam in his pockets. Then he headed to the entry for the boots, coat, and bow and arrows he'd left by the door.

It was just after five a.m. as he stepped outside and closed the back door behind him. He breathed deeply. The sky was taking on the first pink light of dawn.

Kayden looked around with appreciation as he made his way along the back of the house and struck out across the pasture. He knew where he was going, because he'd scouted it out many times before. The only part he was unsure of was where to strike the mountain with his Runestaff to open the portal. Finding the right spot might take some time.

He passed a herd of the Charolais cattle his family

raised. They were lying on a hilltop to take advantage of any cool breezes that might ward off some of the mosquitoes and black flies that plagued them during the summer months. The animals ignored his passage.

Although he had inherited Gran's ability to speak with animals in Erinbourne, he couldn't communicate with them on this side of the portal. He'd tried. And he'd felt pretty stupid when he'd been caught by his Gran, trying to carry on a conversation with a cow, until she explained some things didn't work quite the same way here.

He chuckled, remembering those first days after his adventure in Erinbourne had ended, and he'd returned to normal life in Canada.

Fishing out the apple, he bit into it with a crunch and wiped the juice from his chin with a sleeve. He wasn't planning to stop before he reached the mountain. It would take him about three hours if he hurried. Tossing away the core, he noted that the ground was rising sharply.

He dug his staff into the earth and strode on, imagining the welcome he'd receive when he knocked on the locked gate to Durgot's small realm at the center of what he knew to be called the Ildune Mountain. At least, that was what it was called in Erinbourne.

A forest loomed in front of him, and ducking his head he plunged within, parting the low hanging branches with one hand and gripping his runestaff with the other. He breathed in the pungent scent of the pine. The bow, slung across his back, hindered him a little. While fallen trees and thick, springy mosses slowed him down, but overall Kayden thought he was making good time.

He consulted a watch that had been his father's. There was no point in bringing his cell phone, as it wouldn't work beyond the portal. He'd hidden it in his room, so his parents wouldn't wonder why he'd left it behind. Technology was non-existent where he was going. It was like walking back into the fifteenth century.

Finally, the trees thinned ahead of him and he knew he was almost there. He came out the other side of the tall, straight pines, and was faced with a climb over fallen rocks and thick shale to reach the mountain face. Sliding down, sometimes further than he moved up, he fought his way to the skirt of the mountain and stood panting and leaning on his staff.

Now to find the hidden notch to strike with his runestaff. He remembered there was a huge boulder next to the portal that, if he squinted at it, resembled the head of a dog. It was to that spot that he manoeuvered now. Then, he began searching the mountain face with his fingers, hoping to find the small indentation. Shrugging out of his pack, he let it drop to earth as he moved along the rock, centimeter by centimeter, looking for a needle in a haystack.

Nothing. After an hour of exploring, he flopped against the boulder and wiped his brow. It was noon and the sun was hot. He unwrapped a sandwich and ate it thoughtfully, scrutinising the expanse of rock before him. As he washed the last bite down with a cold gulp of water, he realized what he'd been doing wrong.

He crumpled the plastic wrapping and shoved it into his pocket. Then shouldering the backpack and his bow, he grasped his staff, and held it in front of him. He turned it so he could clearly see the image of a mountain near the tip and concentrated on what he needed, the portal.

The staff came to life for the first time in three years. It shivered, as though waking from a long sleep, and then the image Kayden regarded began to glow with a brightness that was noticeable even in the bright sun of midday.

He smiled with satisfaction, willing the crevice in the rock to reveal itself and allow him entrance into the world beyond its gates.

With a clap like thunder, a jagged fissure split the rock vertically, glimmering as though a bolt of lightning were inlaid in the stone. Moving toward the fracture, Kayden saw the tiny depression off to one side. With both hands, he raised the staff high over his head, lunged forward, and struck the dent with all his might. The fissure cracked wide open, each edge blazing with shimmering light.

Grinning broadly, Kayden stepped through.

Behind him, the aperture slammed shut with a resounding boom. Apart from some dust that sifted onto his hair, everything was still. He was in complete darkness, listening for the distant sounds of the Enchanted River. The water ran around the interior of this mountain to protect the portal from all who might seek to pass without leave.

Concentrating on the rune he could feel at the tip of the staff, he called upon it for light. He was rewarded with the glowing image of a sun that soon grew bright, illuminating the familiar, round cavity hewn from the rock where he now stood.

"It's great to be back!" Kayden said, his voice echoing in the chamber.

He set off along the narrow corridor leading down into the bowels of the mountain. Despite the unevenness of the passage, he strode with a sure step, and soon reached the edge of the Enchanted River. It gurgled at his toes. He raised his runestaff into the air as he had seen Durgot do and focused his thoughts on what he needed at that moment —a bridge.

The staff leapt from his hand, contorting in mid-air, growing and adding to itself as it stretched out across the dark rushing waters of the stream, and fell with a thump to span its width. Kayden extended a foot to test it, since he'd never done this himself. The waters were dangerous, but the makeshift bridge seemed strong, and he hurried across.

Kayden looked down, only for a moment, at the waters that rose in white-capped waves to seek his feet. He knew from experience that if only one drop of that water touched him, every memory he possessed would be blotted from existence.

He stepped onto the other side and turned to stretch out his arm, willing the runestaff to return to him. The bridge reared away from the opposite side and swept into the air, folding onto itself until it was once more the unassuming runestaff.

As it flew into his waiting hand, Kayden realized that he had one last hurdle to jump before arriving at Durgot's gate. He craned his neck to look at the sheer rock wall he must climb in order to reach the marble door high above. Durgot had used his charmed boussole to trigger hidden steps, but Kayden didn't have one. He'd carried the flat silver object for a while, but had given it back to Durgot once they returned from the quest. How was he going to get up there?

Kayden crouched down, well away from the stream, to think. He hadn't thought to bring rope. Besides, there was nothing to loop it around if he had one. He was stumped and leaned against the cold, damp wall.

Could he get this close and fail to reach Durgot? It was unthinkable.

Grab your copy...
vinci-books.com/thelegacy

www.ingramcontent.com/pod-product-compliance
Lightning Source LLC
Chambersburg PA
CBHW01220703726
47494CB00023B/2560